PRAISE FOR

Nonna Maria and the Case of the Missing Bride

"An utterly delightful tale starring one of the most charming amateur sleuths ever created, *Nonna Maria and the Case of the Missing Bride* is so delicious it will make you want to pack your bags and move to Italy!"

—TESS GERRITSEN, *New York Times* bestselling author of *Listen to Me*

"The brilliant Lorenzo Carcaterra has created his own irresistible genre: the literary cozy. I fell in love with this wonderfully lyrical and completely entertaining novel, and most of all its instantly iconic heroine. Nonna Maria is Miss Marple and Sherlock Holmes combined into one wise and unforgettable character. Touching, charming, and delightful—do not miss this!"

—*USA Today* bestselling author HANK PHILLIPPI RYAN

"Lorenzo Carcaterra has written a suspenseful tale while bringing the history, traditions, and colorful characters of the island of Ischia to life. The indomitable Nonna Maria shines throughout. Bravo!"

—CAMILLA TRINCHIERI, author of the Tuscan Mystery series

"Nostalgia for Ischia's simpler way of life, nearly lost in the face of the fast-paced modern world, combines successfully with a suspenseful plot and a feisty heroine who's as kind as she is steely."

—*Booklist*

PRAISE FOR

Lorenzo Carcaterra

"One of the all-time greats." —JEFFERY DEAVER, #1 international
bestselling author of the Lincoln Rhyme series

"One of my favorite writers in the world."
—LISA SCOTTOLINE, *New York Times*
bestselling author of *Someone Knows*

"A writer who has earned his spot at the top echelon of suspense
masters . . . Lorenzo Carcaterra is simply the best."
—STEVE BERRY, *New York Times*
bestselling author of the Cotton Malone series

"Lorenzo Carcaterra knows gritty storytelling."
—ALAFAIR BURKE, *New York Times* bestselling author of *Find Me*

"Carcaterra writes with the passion of Styron, the guts of Mailer, and
the sting of James M. Cain."
—WILLIAM DIEHL, *New York Times* bestselling author of *Primal Fear*

NONNA MARIA

and the Case of the Missing Bride

BY LORENZO CARCATERRA

A Safe Place:
The True Story of a Father, a Son, a Murder

Sleepers

Apaches

Gangster

Street Boys

Paradise City

Chasers

Midnight Angels

The Wolf

Tin Badges

Payback

Three Dreamers

Nonna Maria and the Case of the Missing Bride

SHORT STORY

The Vulture's Game

NONNA MARIA

and the Case of the Missing Bride

A NOVEL

LORENZO CARCATERRA

BANTAM

2023 Bantam Books Trade Paperback Edition

Published in the United States by Bantam Books, an imprint of Random House, a division of Penguin Random House LLC, New York.

BANTAM BOOKS is a registered trademark and the B colophon is a trademark of Penguin Random House LLC.

Originally published in hardcover in the United States by Bantam Books, an imprint of Random House, a division of Penguin Random House LLC, in 2022.

This book contains an excerpt from the forthcoming book *Nonna Maria and the Case of the Stolen Necklace* by Lorenzo Carcaterra. This excerpt has been set for this edition only and may not reflect the final content of the forthcoming edition.

LIBRARY OF CONGRESS CATALOGING-IN-PUBLICATION DATA
Names: Carcaterra, Lorenzo, author.
Title: Nonna Maria and the case of the missing bride: a novel / Lorenzo Carcaterra.
Description: New York: Bantam Books, [2022] Identifiers: LCCN 2021037707 (print)
| LCCN 2021037708 (ebook) |
ISBN 9780399177644 (trade paperback) | ISBN 9780399177637 (ebook)
Subjects: LCGFT: Cozy mysteries. | Novels. Classification: LCC PS3553.A653 N66
2022 (print) | LCC PS3553.A653 (ebook) | DDC 813/.54—dc23
LC record available at lccn.loc.gov/2021037707
LC ebook record available at lccn.loc.gov/2021037708

Printed in the United States of America on acid-free paper

randomhousebooks.com

1st Printing

Book design by Fritz Metsch

This one is for Mary Ellen Theresa Keating.
Beautiful, smart, generous, loving, caring, tough,
funny, kind, with warm eyes that could melt the heart
of any man. She is so very easy to love. Nonna Maria
would welcome her in her company
with open arms.

NONNA MARIA

and the Case of the Missing Bride

1.

NONNA MARIA POURED herself a hot cup of espresso, her third of the morning, and gazed out the small kitchen window of her two-story white stone home. She then picked up a folded hand towel and brought the espresso pot into the dining room and rested it on a round silver tray. She pulled back a thick wooden chair and sat down. She rested her hands on the table and glanced at the young woman sitting across from her. There was an empty cup resting next to the woman's right arm.

"I'm sorry to have come this early," the woman said. She couldn't have been much older than nineteen, her low voice still cradling the path between teenager and adult. "I should have called first."

"I don't have a phone," Nonna Maria said. "And it's never too early or too late to come see me. The coffee's still hot and a warm cup will do you good."

The woman glanced at the coffeepot and shook her head. "I wouldn't mind a glass of water," she said. "If it's not too much of a bother."

"Water's only good for plants," Nonna Maria said. "Have

some coffee instead; it will help you relax and make it easier for you to tell me why you came to see me."

Nonna Maria lifted the espresso pot and waited as the woman slid her empty cup closer to her. She filled the cup and then passed the sugar bowl across the table. "It's better with sugar," she said. "Two teaspoons are what most people prefer. I like three, myself. My nephew has asked me many times to cut back. But, then, he's a doctor, and part of his job is to tell me to cut back on what I like to eat and drink."

The woman smiled for the first time since she entered Nonna Maria's house. It was the last house in a row of four similar houses in a small piazza facing a white rock wall, with pockets of black stains on the base, the result of too many years enduring too many rainstorms. The house was less than half a block from the local beach, a beach Nonna Maria had never once visited.

The woman took a sip of the coffee, rested her cup on the table, and then settled back in her chair. She looked like many of the local girls of the island. Her hair was dark and thick, running along the sides of her face; occasionally a few loose strands would rest next to one of her cheeks and she would flick them back with a quick flip of her head. Her eyes were dark as coal and her skin was brown from many summers spent under a hot sun.

"I'm so afraid, Nonna Maria," she said in a quivering voice. "I've put myself in a horrible position and don't know how to get out of it, not without causing my parents, my family, great expense and even greater embarrassment."

"Does it have anything to do with your upcoming wedding?" Nonna Maria asked. She sat with her gnarled hands flat on the wood table, her dark eyes taking in the young woman sitting across from her. "And the man you've chosen to marry?"

The woman stared at Nonna Maria for several seconds and then nodded. "It's true what they say about you," the woman said, meekly attempting a smile. "You *do* know everything that happens on this island."

Nonna Maria shook her head and gave her a half smile. "I don't know everything," she said. "I only know what I hear. And on an island filled with people who love to talk, especially about matters that don't concern them, I hear quite a bit."

Nonna Maria stood and walked toward the front door, a slight limp causing her to favor her right leg. She was wearing the widow's black, a heavy full-length skirt and a long-sleeved blouse; her thick white hair was done up in a bun, curled and pinned to the top of her head with an array of black pins. "Come," she said to the young woman, "and walk with me up to Via Roma. I want to visit one of my daughters. She had minor surgery the other day and my nephew—the doctor I spoke about earlier—wants to make sure she gets enough to eat, and he assigned the task to me. And while we walk, you can tell me why you don't want to marry this man, Andrea Bartoli."

The woman pushed back her chair, stood, and walked toward Nonna Maria. "You even know his name," she said, not bothering to hide her surprise.

"As I told you," Nonna Maria said, "I hear many things without the need to ask many questions. All that's needed is for me to listen."

"And what is it they say about me and the man I'm supposed to marry?" the young woman asked.

"They say, Anna," Nonna Maria said, referring to the young woman by her name for the first time, "that you're marrying not out of love but out of fear, for yourself and for your family."

"And do you believe what they say?"

"Idle talk is just that, talk," Nonna Maria said. "I'll believe it when you tell me it's more than that."

"And if it is?" Anna asked.

Nonna Maria opened the front door and waited for Anna to approach the entryway. "Then I will be there to help you," she said.

2.

NONNA MARIA HAD been a widow for twenty-five years. She was in her early seventies, though few on the island were certain as to her exact age and all knew it best not to ask. Her late husband, Gabriel, was a much-beloved shepherd, who tended to his flock and donated clothes, milk, and meat to those most in need. They had married young and raised a family of seven through good years and difficult ones. They had lost a grown son and an infant grandson to disease and another grandson in a car accident but always managed to keep the family united during those turbulent times.

Except for the occasional wedding and far too many funerals in Naples, Nonna Maria never left her home of Ischia. She had watched with silent amazement as Ischia, eighteen miles off the coast of Naples, had, over the course of her life, grown from an impoverished island to a magnet for thousands of tourists who filled its streets. During the height of the summer season, they crammed into both five-star hotels and small motels, while the beaches and spas were filled to capacity during the day and restaurants and clubs stayed open till nearly sunrise to accommodate all the customers. In a short span of time, many of the locals of the island went from living in despair and poverty to earning enough to keep their families well fed and financially secure.

Ischia has a population of sixty-five thousand, spread across five boroughs and 18 square miles. The island has long been famous for its rich thermal waters, their strength derived from the volcanic soil on which the island is built. For centuries, wealthy Northern Italians flocked to Ischia to cure their bodily ills and enjoy a sun-drenched break from life. Michelangelo built a house on the island, and Julius Caesar traveled there to take the mud baths to help heal his body after years in combat.

It is also an island that caught the eyes of filmmakers, both American and Italian. The Italian director Vittorio De Sica vacationed there, often in the company of his friends and frequent stars of his films, Marcello Mastroianni and Sophia Loren. The director Billy Wilder and the actor Jack Lemmon so loved their time on Ischia that they decided to film a movie entirely on the island, using many of the locals as extras and in small parts. The 1972 movie—*Avanti!*—brought the island a bit of notoriety and led to a few more tourists coming to visit.

But it was one movie in particular that made the island a mecca of tourism, one that nearly bankrupted a studio and caused an international stir as the press went into a fever pitch covering a romance between its two leading actors, Richard Burton and Elizabeth Taylor. The press attention the movie, *Cleopatra*, brought to the island has now long been forgotten. But the constant barrage of photos taken of the couple with the beauty of the island behind them led to a squadron of hotel and restaurant developers realizing this was an island ripe for investment. By the late sixties and early seventies, the quiet island of Ischia was packed with more than five hundred thousand visitors during the summer months.

None of this mattered to Nonna Maria.

To her, the island was not a tourist destination. It was her home. She was a familiar presence in the port area and was known and trusted by all who lived there. These were her people, young and old, and they had come to lean on her for advice and help during difficult times. She became the one they turned to when marital disputes needed to be resolved, when the time came to bring a family feud to an end, when a business was in distress and wise counsel was required.

Nonna Maria made wide use of her network of friends and family, spread throughout the entire island and reaching as far as Naples and Rome, a city she had never once visited. She was smart, listened to all sides of an argument, and never rushed to judgment. Nonna Maria was the person the locals of Ischia turned to first to guide them through troubled waters. She was their North Star and she never failed them.

Sometimes, they even turned to Nonna Maria with issues that should be brought to the attention of the local carabinieri and not a widow with a bad right leg. The carabinieri are respected and admired throughout Italy, and Ischia was no exception. But there was always a bit of hesitation to go to them for help. The reasoning behind such thinking was simple: The carabinieri in Ischia were from other cities, often from Northern Italy, and not men and women the locals had grown up around. They would often serve six months, sometimes a year, on the island and then be transferred to another place, replaced by another strange face. Not being from the island, the carabinieri might not understand how to negotiate a festering family feud or how a minor slight could turn into a physical altercation. It was far better to turn to a local to solve such issues.

"We turn to those we know when there are problems," Gaspare Mangini once told a young carabiniere who stopped by his café, La Dolce Sosta. "Like the time my son Carlo thought his Vespa had been stolen. That normally would be something you report to the carabinieri. But I have known Nonna Maria since I was old enough to walk. I sent him to see her. She knew what the Vespa meant to him. It was a gift from his grandmother, and she gave it to him a week before she died. That Vespa was his link to her, and he couldn't stand the idea of losing it. It took Nonna Maria two days to find the Vespa. It wasn't stolen. There had been an accident the night it went missing, several people injured in a car that slid into a ravine, about twelve miles from our home. A relative of one of our neighbors was one of the injured. Her nephew, in a panic and wanting to get there as fast as he could, kick-started Carlo's Vespa and drove it up to the site. Nonna Maria knew the family and realized the boy would return the Vespa as soon as his aunt was out of danger. If we had brought in the carabinieri, there would have been paperwork and possibly charges against the young man. Instead, an apology and a handshake brought an end to the situation. Thanks to Nonna Maria."

3.

PASQUALE FAVORINI EASED his tour boat into the mouth of Porto d'Ischia harbor. He had been crossing the waters surrounding the island since he was a boy of fourteen and his father, Domenico, had passed the captain's wheel to him. He was now one week shy of his eighty-fifth birthday and had no desire to give up his life on the open sea. The rigors and the routine of the life were as much a part of him as the ever-present pipe tucked in the corner of his mouth. He didn't care much for the tourists who crowded onto his boat for each of the three ninety-minute tours he would do each day during the season, plus the additional weekly one done under a starlit sky and ending with a champagne breakfast at the Maronti beach.

The tours paid his salary and for the fuel and upkeep of his beloved boat, the *Lucia Bianca*. It was his grandmother's name, and he considered the boat as much a part of his family as his wife, Fernanda, his three grown daughters, and his six grandchildren. And family it would always remain, though none of his children or their husbands had any desire to make a life as a tour-boat captain, choosing instead to leave the island and make their home and living in Northern cities.

While Pasquale piloted the boat and stared out at the sun-soaked sea he had loved his entire life, he left the tours to his first mate, Giovanni Buonopana. The young man was in his early twenties and was ambitious and hardworking and kept the tourists entertained with his tales about the island's history—most of them true, others embellished just enough to still be believable. They had been together for three years, and in that time Buonopana was content to play tour guide, working for a meager salary and the tips he shared with the captain. He loved the old captain and felt that he would one day take command of Pasquale's beloved *Lucia Bianca*.

But Pasquale had no intention of retiring. He was in fine health for his age, still able to handle the boat through heavy seas or calm waters. His skin was rough and tanned, from the decades spent at his trade. His upper body was still muscular, though slowed by stiffness and joint pain. His once-thick head of hair the color of night had thinned and was now tinged with streaks of white, and, after a long day on the water, he felt the bones of his legs ache more than they ever had. But he still took pride in prepping the boat for its daily runs and then washing and storing her gear as their day came to an end. He worked alongside his beloved dog, Pippo, a mini-Aussie who followed him everywhere and with whom he shared both his breakfast and lunch.

Pasquale docked the boat, watched as Buonopana tossed thick ropes around two rusty iron pilings and shut the engines down. He stepped down from the captain's perch, Pippo fast on his heels, Buonopana waiting for both of them to disembark.

Pasquale stepped off the boat and pulled a small box of

matches from the front pocket of his thick corduroy pants and lit his pipe. "We have an early tour tomorrow," he said to Buonopana, "and need to leave by eight. The tourists should be lined up around seven-thirty, maybe earlier. The office said we should expect a full load, at least forty, maybe a few extra stragglers will join the group."

"That will leave me only a few hours to prep the boat," Buonopana said. "I might as well spend the night in the cabin. We're filling in for Salvatore tonight, doing the midnight tour, remember?"

"I didn't forget," Pasquale said. "Though to be honest, I wish he had asked someone else to take his slot. Three tours in one day is more than enough for us."

"You look tired, Pasquale," Buonopana said. "Maybe you should start taking a day off each week. I can handle both the boat and the tour. And we'll still divide the tips same as always."

"You worry about me more than my wife and children do," Pasquale said. "So long as I can breathe, no one but me takes the wheel of the *Lucia Bianca*. It's what keeps me alive."

"You're the oldest captain on these waters, Pasquale," Buonopana said. "And still the best one. I just want to help you. You let me run the boat a few times each week, it will keep you stronger through the season. We'll be doing each other a favor."

"You want to do me a favor?" Pasquale said. "Then come with me and Pippo and join us for dinner. There's a delicious meal waiting for the three of us."

"I don't want to be a bother to you or to your wife," Buonopana said. "It's more than enough that she makes me lunch every day. You should go home and be with your family."

"You are part of my family," Pasquale said. "You have been since you first started working with me. I promised your father I would look after you, and I have done my best in that regard. But the truth is, it is you that has been looking after me all these years. You are as much one of my children as my own daughters."

Buonopana gazed at the old man and the dog as they made their way up the slight incline, past two gelato shops and a hotel, and nodded. "I feel the same about you. And, yes, I will join you for dinner. On one condition."

Pasquale turned and looked at Buonopana. "What is it?"

"That we stop at Naturischia and you let me buy some wine for us to enjoy with the great meal that awaits," Buonopana said.

Pasquale smiled. "Have you ever known anyone from Ischia to refuse a bottle of wine?" he asked.

4.

"I WAS SITTING on that bench the day we first met," Anna said. She was walking arm in arm with Nonna Maria in the gardens abutting the rear of the Bar Calise. The lush gardens, surrounded by thick bushes, were mostly used by early-morning joggers who enjoyed their runs on the soft dirt paths, shaded overhead by rows of pine trees. In the late evenings, the gardens were coveted by lovers young and old, a peaceful and secluded place to listen to the music flowing from the piano and microphone of Aldo Poli, the resident singer at the Bar Calise.

"You would not be the first woman to be approached by a man in these gardens," Nonna Maria said. "Nor the last. Couples have met here to fall in, and sometimes out, of love since I was a child. And even in the years before that."

"He asked if I minded if he sat down, and I didn't and we began talking," Anna said. "It was very casual and polite. He told me he was visiting the island for the first time and was trying to see as much as he could in the short time he would be here."

"Did he tell you where he was from?" Nonna Maria asked.

Anna shook her head. "I didn't ask," she said. "From the

way he spoke, it sounded as if he was from somewhere in the North. He didn't speak in our dialect or any from other parts of the South. He looked and sounded like a well-educated, well-mannered man on vacation."

"He looked and sounded how he wanted you to think he looked and sounded," Nonna Maria said.

"Yes," Anna said. "But he was charming and seemed without pretense. So, when he asked if I wanted to join him for a gelato at the Bar Calise, I went along. Looking back, I should have said no and gone on my way. If there's anyone to blame about the situation I find myself in, it's me."

"If mistakes are to be made, they are best made when we are young," Nonna Maria said. "When you went to the bar, did you find a table or did you order your gelato at the counter?"

"It was crowded, as it always is during the summer, especially when Aldo Poli is at the piano as he was that night," Anna said. "But we managed to find a table in a corner in the back, on the other side of the entrance."

"Did a waiter take your order, or did this man, Bartoli, go and get your gelato?" Nonna Maria asked.

"We waited a few minutes for a waiter to come to our table," Anna said. "But when one didn't look our way, he went into the bar to get our order."

"And you didn't go with him?"

Anna shook her head. "No," she said. "He told me to sit and enjoy the music. He wasn't gone long. No more than five minutes."

They were heading out of the garden now and walking

toward Ischia Ponte, the cobblestone streets sloping down, the imposing structure of the Castello Aragonese looming in the distance. "You probably ordered a chocolate gelato," Nonna Maria said to Anna. "But Bartoli didn't get himself a gelato. He came back to the table with something else."

Anna stopped and turned to face Nonna Maria. "Yes," she said. "He said he wanted an iced espresso instead. But how did you know that?"

"What young girl doesn't like a chocolate gelato?" Nonna Maria said. "And Bartoli made sure to get you a double scoop, the more for you to enjoy."

"That's right," Anna said. "He said it was a warm night and it would help cool me off. And I didn't want him to feel bad, so I ate both scoops. He sat back, sipped his coffee, and smiled at me the whole time."

"How did you feel after you had finished the gelato?" Nonna Maria asked.

"A little light-headed," Anna said. "I thought maybe it was because of the warm night and the crowded bar. I really don't remember much else about that night. It's been one big blur since then. At least it was until a few days ago."

"It means it's beginning to wear off," Nonna Maria said.

"What is?"

Nonna Maria ignored the question. "How long ago was this first meeting?" she asked.

"This coming Tuesday will be four weeks," Anna said.

"And do you remember all that happened during those weeks?" Nonna Maria asked. "Bringing Bartoli to your home, introducing him to your family? Going out on dates with him? Spending most of your days in his company? Agreeing to become his wife?"

Anna lowered her head. "No, Nonna Maria," she said, her eyes now moist with fresh tears. "I don't remember much, other than a few scattered words and places where we went. What have I done? What have I done to my family?"

Nonna Maria reached out her arms for the young woman and embraced her. "You've done nothing wrong, my sweet child," she said. "But there can be no errors in what you do over the next several days. You must act with care and without a word to anyone. No one must know."

Anna released the embrace, wiped at her tears, and nodded. "What is it you need me to do?" she asked.

"I want you to disappear," Nonna Maria said.

5.

LATER THAT MORNING, Nonna Maria walked down the long sloping street from her home to the hub of the port. It was—as it always was this time of year, the heart of the summer season—a scene of organized chaos. Tourists emerging from hydrofoils and large boats, their luggage crammed onto iron carts pulled by muscular and sweat-stained young men, working for tips and the occasional pack of cigarettes. Buses and taxicabs were lined in neat rows, drivers and guides standing in front of them holding up signs for the tourists to see, waiting to take them to their hotel or villa, for the start of their vacation.

The small counter of the coffee bar was packed with workers eager for a fresh cup of coffee or their first taste of a morning pastry. The dozen tables scattered around the small piazza facing the bar were also filled, mostly with locals taking in the scene they had gotten used to in the years since the island had grown in popularity.

The stout middle-aged woman behind the counter of the bar smiled and waved when she spotted Nonna Maria. "Do you have time for a coffee?" she asked.

"Is it as good as the one I make in my kitchen?" Nonna Maria asked.

The stout woman laughed out loud and shook her head. "Not even close, Nonna Maria," she said. "If I could make coffee as good as yours I would be able to charge the tourists three times what they're paying."

"I would show you how I make it," Nonna Maria said, moving past the bar, "but some things we need to keep a secret."

Nonna Maria found the man she was looking for leaning against the front of a large, freshly washed tour bus. He was a handsome middle-aged man with tanned arms and face, his arms crossed over the front of his button-down blue denim shirt, the sleeves rolled to the elbow. He smiled when he saw Nonna Maria approach.

"Please don't tell me you need to find another home for a lost cat," he said as she stepped up closer, carefully dodging a black Vespa with two teenagers on board, heading toward Campagna. "The last one you gave me still keeps me up nights with his purring and prowling. And the beautiful tourists who I would want to bring home with me all tell me they're allergic to cats. He's destroyed any chance I have at a social life, my Bruno has."

"He's better company for you, Mario," Nonna Maria said. "And, in the long run, a lot less trouble."

Mario Scaovoni was known throughout Ischia as the King of the Port. He was in his early forties and had started his tour business with two cabs when he was barely old enough to get a license. Over the years, he built the business to where it now included a fleet of fourteen buses and a dozen vans and cabs. He also owned four tour boats and had partial interest in several restaurants and three of the island's five-star hotels. He worked endlessly, never seemed to tire, and employed a staff of one hundred twenty-five locals the year round. Nonna Maria had known him since he was an infant. His parents, Graziella and Francesco, were close friends of hers who owned a fruit stand steps from her home.

Mario was the eyes and ears of the port and could distinguish in a blink of an eye the fresh-faced tourist from the ones who had been coming to Ischia for decades. "One of the buses on the far end will be heading out for a tour of the island in a few minutes," he said to her. "There's one empty seat. It's yours if you're interested. Might do you some good."

"Are you doing the tour?" she asked.

"I don't usually anymore," Mario said. "I leave that to the more-experienced guides, the ones who know the real history of the island. When I do them, I talk about whatever pops into my head. Whether it's true or not. I'm not here to educate them, Nonna Maria. Just to show them a good time. That's what keeps them coming back year after year. The history they can get out of a book."

"I know all the history of the island I need to know," Nonna Maria said. "But a good story is always hard to pass up."

"In that case, I will be honored to serve as your tour guide," Mario said. "Is there any particular story you'd like to hear?"

"I would," Nonna Maria said. "But it's a personal one. I'm not sure you want to share it with a busload of tourists."

Mario smiled and tilted his head at Nonna Maria. "So, you didn't just come down here to say hello to an old friend. You need information. I tell you, Nonna Maria, the local carabinieri are making a big mistake not putting you on their payroll."

"If you don't want to tell the story, you don't have to," Nonna Maria said. "I won't ask you to do anything that will make you uncomfortable."

"What is the story you would like me to tell?" Mario asked.

"The one about La Fattura," Nonna Maria said.

Mario started to walk toward the bus on the far end of the line. Nonna Maria followed. "That is a good one," he said. "And I don't mind telling it. Young man marries a woman he barely knows and, less than a week after the wedding, wakes up in a cold sweat, not knowing who he married or why. That will entertain them better than me pointing out a side of a mountain that Saint Anthony kept from falling and killing the good people of the port during an earthquake that happened centuries ago."

"That's true," Nonna Maria said. "And it might also tell them a little about the history of the island. The *real* history."

"And that this story happened to me makes it even better for them to hear," Mario said.

"What happened to you happened years ago, when you were much younger," Nonna Maria said. "Do you wonder if such things happen today?"

"You hear talk of it now and then," Mario said. "You meet a pretty girl at a party or a friend asks you to walk a girl home as a favor. You get to her house, she asks you to come in and meet her sister. You then find yourself in a stranger's home. From there, anything is possible. Today as much as it was years ago."

"They offered you a drink and you took it," Nonna Maria said.

Mario nodded. "That's right. And before I knew it, I was married to a woman I barely knew."

"The same situation happened to my youngest son, as you are well aware," Nonna Maria said. "My mother had warned me about never taking anything from anyone I didn't know, especially if they weren't drinking or eating it themselves. She called it La Fattura and said it was a practice brought here centuries ago. I passed that lesson on to my children. All but one listened and took it to heart."

"Something is put in the drink or the food," Mario said. "I never learned what it was, but I know one thing. You are not yourself after that and are put into a place you would never be in if your mind was right."

"There were many who found themselves in situations like that," Nonna Maria said. "But I haven't heard about it happening for a long time."

"I haven't heard about it for a while, either," Mario said. "Last one was maybe eight, ten years ago. Neri, the pharmacist's son, the one from Lacco Ameno, woke up married to a woman whose name he didn't even know."

Nonna Maria turned to look at the traffic moving in and out of the port. The large boats crammed with cars and tourists. The hydrofoils packed with tired and eager men, women, and children, all anxious to get on land and bring their journey to an end. Traffic lanes on both sides of the street slowed to a crawl.

"It may have left us for a while," Nonna Maria said, turning back to face Mario. "But now I think it might be back. The curse is back."

6.

NONNA MARIA WAS taught at a young age about the many traditions, curses, and folklore that had long existed on the island of Ischia. She believed in a few and discounted others but was aware of them all. For example, she knew that a loaf of bread on her table must always be turned faceup; otherwise, bad luck would follow. And that birds—either pets or brought in by a guest—were never allowed in her home, for the same reason. And she never walked in the path of an empty hearse; otherwise, death would soon come calling for her.

Of the many spells, curses, and traditions Nonna Maria learned about as a child, the one she heard about the most was that of La Fattura. It was an herbal potion that, if given to an unsuspecting man or woman, would cause them to fall under a spell lasting long enough for them to agree to marry the person chosen.

Nonna Maria warned her own children many times to never take any drink from a stranger and if they found themselves in someone's home to never accept anything to eat or drink that the people offering were not themselves drinking from the same jug or eating from the same pot. She had, in her many years, seen a number of marriages occur only to see them dissolve once one of the parties allegedly came out from under the spell of La Fattura.

Nonna Maria was not, as a rule, a superstitious woman. But she was a careful one and was aware that there were a small number of people on the island who earned money practicing the dark arts, handed down to them from generations long since buried.

She poured herself a fresh cup of coffee and sat back in her chair, gazing out the window of her home. The dining room was sparsely furnished, consisting of a table, four chairs, a small couch, and a cot nestled in one corner. The walls were adorned with only two photos, encased in large wooden frames—one was of her late husband and the other of a son who died at too young an age. The two photos faced each other from opposing white stucco walls.

Nonna Maria was focused on Anna. Was she simply a young woman who was regretting a rash decision to marry a man she barely knew and looking for an excuse? Or had she indeed been put under the spell of La Fattura?

She thought back to ten years earlier, when her youngest son, Franco, was on his honeymoon in Venice, married to a woman he had known less than two weeks. Upon his return to Ischia, he told his mother how in the middle of the night he jumped to his feet from the bed, his body awash in a cold sweat, not knowing where he was and barely recognizing the woman who had been asleep by his side.

"It could have been just a dream," Nonna Maria had said to her son on his first day back.

"It wasn't a dream I had, Mama," Franco said. "It's a nightmare I'm living each and every day. I still don't remember how I find myself married to a woman I barely know, let alone love."

"But you knew her," Nonna Maria said. "Before you rushed headfirst like a stubborn mule into marriage. You did know this woman."

Franco nodded. "I remember meeting her," he said. "My friend Alberto was dating Carmella at the time, and she had a friend visiting from Naples. Alberto asked if I would be kind enough to join them for dinner and a movie. This way, the young lady, Paola, would not feel left out."

"And you went to the dinner and the movie?"

"Yes," Franco said. "Afterward, Alberto and Carmella went for a walk on the Lido and I took Paola to the place where she was staying."

"Did you go in?" Nonna Maria asked. "Or did you say buona sera at the door?"

"I was going to leave," Franco said. "But there was a man on the terrace smoking a cigarette—her uncle, I think. He asked me to come up and have a drink with him. And so I went into the house."

"Did he drink with you?" Nonna Maria asked her son. "This man, did he pour himself a drink from the same pitcher that he poured yours?"

Franco shook his head. "He already had a glass," he said. "It wasn't wine. It was a dark liquid. Either a Fernet or an Averna."

"And what did he pour for you?"

"A large glass of red wine," Franco said. "He said it was a Super Tuscan and he had just opened a fresh bottle."

"How did it taste?"

"It was strong and bitter and burned my throat," Franco said. "I had never had a Super Tuscan. I've only had island wine, which is not very strong. So I just assumed that's what Super Tuscans tasted like. I didn't want to be rude, so I finished the glass and said my good night. To him and to the girl."

"The girl that's now your wife," Nonna Maria said.

"I don't remember anything else about that night," Franco said. "I don't remember anything until I jumped out of the hotel bed in Venice."

Nonna Maria finished the last of her coffee, stood, and walked to the kitchen, resting the cup and saucer in the sink. Franco had been one of the lucky ones. He had the marriage annulled less than a month after they were wed. The bride's family originally sought a cash settlement, but Nonna Maria enlisted the aid of a local priest, Don Nicola, and at his request a meeting was arranged. At that meeting, Don Nicola stood in front of both families, took a glass from the table, and filled it with red wine. Then he reached into his pockets and pulled out a packet of herbs and a small vial of a red liquid and poured both into the glass of wine. He lifted the glass and swirled the mixture together. Then he sat down and nodded to Nonna Maria.

Nonna Maria looked across the table at the uncle who had given her son a glass of wine. "You want money in return for my son's freedom from this marriage," she said. "Fine. I'll pay any sum you request. But first you drink the wine that Don Nicola prepared for you. Drink until the glass is empty."

The uncle shook his head. "That would be crazy," he said.

"I don't know what he put in that glass. I would be a fool to drink it."

"It could be he added fresh herbs and local wine to lighten the taste," Nonna Maria said. "In which case it's a harmless drink. Or he added what you added to my son's glass. You have a choice. Which is more than you gave my son."

The man cupped the glass in his hands for several moments, staring at Nonna Maria. He then released the glass and set it aside. "I'll sign the papers," he said. "The marriage between your son and my niece will be as if it never existed."

Nonna Maria nodded. "There's one other thing you must do," she said. "After you sign the papers."

"What?" he asked.

"You leave the island," Nonna Maria said. "All of you. Leave and never return. The carabinieri know what you've done, and they will be watching, should you decide to return. And the Church knows about you, and they will be watching. And most important of all, I know about you, and I will always be watching."

Nonna Maria stepped out of her kitchen and walked toward the open door of her house. She reached into a large bowl resting on the table and grabbed a number of sweet candies and put them in the front pockets of her widow's dress. She never knew when she would run into a grandchild, and having them reach for a candy from her dress was a ritual that must be observed.

She stepped out into the warm, humid day and made her way down the circular iron stairs.

It was time to learn the truth about Andrea Bartoli.

7.

THE CARABINIERI OFFICE in the port was located near the low-income housing complex known as Casa Popolare. It was a residential area populated by the working poor, those who could not afford to buy homes of their own or who didn't earn enough wages to pay the high rents of an apartment on the island. This was true especially in the port area, where prices had risen in the past several years due to the increased demand of both foreigners and Northerners looking to buy second homes and condos, using them as vacation retreats.

Nonna Maria knew many, if not all, of the residents of Casa Popolare. These were hardworking men and women with large families who did not rent out their apartments in the summer months at exorbitant rates and were not in line to inherit a home or a condo from a relative with means. In years past, when her husband was alive, Nonna Maria would visit these families and hand out clothes and fresh fruits and meats. These days, Nonna Maria was sought out for her advice and counsel on matters residents deemed essential—from housing disputes with local officials to matrimonial matters to long-simmering feuds. And while they could have easily walked into the carabinieri station house to air their complaints, they much preferred the wise judgment of an old and trusted friend.

Nonna Maria was a few buildings removed from the carabinieri headquarters when she was approached by a familiar face, Filomena Castagna. She, too, was a widow, with a daughter and three sons, the youngest of whom, Gennaro, was rumored to have a crush on young Anna, who had instead agreed to marry Andrea Bartoli.

"Have you heard about the wedding?" Filomena asked her. "Between Anna and the stranger?"

"He is a stranger to you, Filomena, and to me," Nonna Maria said. "But not to Anna. She has agreed to marry him. That makes him more than a stranger."

"My son, Gennaro, is heartbroken," Filomena said. "He and Anna have known each other since they were infants. And he thought one day they would make a life together. That's the way it seemed to us, her family and mine, until this Bartoli fellow came into her life."

Nonna Maria nodded. "Did Gennaro go see Anna after he heard about her engagement to Bartoli?"

Filomena shook her head. "He is stubborn, like most men on this island," she said. "He has been sulking like a boy since he found out. He thinks Anna is getting married because Bartoli has money and can give her a better life than she could have if she were married to a hotel baggage handler. And let's be honest, Nonna Maria, there is truth to that."

"Gennaro works hard and makes an honest living," Nonna Maria said. "And he's young still; this is his first real job. Antonio Zapieri owns the hotel where your son now works, and he lives in a villa in Serrara Fontana."

"That's what money gets you," Filomena said.

"But not so long ago, his first job was the same as Gennaro's," Nonna Maria said. "He worked as a baggage handler in the hotel he now owns. Everyone must start somewhere, and for the working poor, that somewhere is always with the lowest-paying job. Gennaro is just beginning his journey. Tell him for me not to lose hope. Hard work always has a way of paying off."

"It will be difficult for him to do," Filomena said, "without his beloved Anna. He is a lost soul, my son. Doesn't eat, sleep, or drink. Just sits and curses the fact he was born so poor it cost him the love of his life."

"She's not married to Bartoli yet," Nonna Maria said. "And if Anna is truly the love of Gennaro's life, as he believes, then there might be a way for the two of them to find each other again."

8.

CAPTAIN PAOLO MURINO of the carabinieri smiled when he spotted Nonna Maria turn the corner of the station house and walk toward his office. He greeted her warmly and pulled out a black leather-back chair for her to sit on. "It's been a while since you paid us a visit," he said, leaning against his desk. "I was beginning to think you'd given up your career as a crime fighter."

"I leave that business to you," Nonna Maria said. "I don't do anything more than help friends who ask for help."

Captain Murino and Nonna Maria treated each other as friendly opponents in a chess match. He had been in command of the carabinieri for five years now, arriving as a young officer from Milan who quickly embraced the pace and traditions of the island. He struggled at first to understand the dialect of the island but soon grew comfortable enough with its cadence and shortened words to speak at length with any of the locals.

He was in his mid-thirties, tall, with light-brown hair, and gave off a warm and welcoming vibe. Two years earlier he had met an island girl who came into the carabinieri office to contest a parking ticket and he fell in love. His future bride, Loretta D'Angelo, lived in Parco Margherita, less than a mile from police headquarters, and the two could often be seen enjoying a quiet lunch together under an awning off the entrance to the station. They were set to be married in the fall, after the end of the summer season.

Captain Murino valued Nonna Maria's opinion and marveled at how she seemed always to know everyone on the island. In the captain's years in charge of the carabinieri stationed in Ischia, Nonna Maria had proven useful to him on a number of investigations. Still, he wished the locals put as much faith in him and the members of his force as they did in an old widow whose trust they held close to their hearts.

"Would you like an espresso?" Captain Murino asked.

"The only coffee I drink comes from my kitchen," Nonna Maria said.

Captain Murino sat in his leather chair and shuffled aside a number of yellow folders. "In that case, let's get down to it. How can I help you today, Nonna Maria? And I must ask you to make it brief; it's a busy morning. I need to leave in a few minutes to head to the port and see if my scuba divers had luck finding a missing tour-boat captain."

Nonna Maria stared for a moment at Captain Murino. "Which tour-boat captain?" she asked.

"The oldest one," Captain Murino said. "Pasquale Favorini. His first mate reported him missing late last night. We think he fell overboard."

"Favorini is my friend, and he can navigate our waters better than any tour-boat captain working the bay," Nonna Maria said. "He was raised on a boat and can bring it into dock blind-folded. He is not a man to fall overboard, no matter the weather or his condition."

"That may have been true in earlier times," Captain Murino said. "But he should have retired years ago. Especially given how much he likes his wine."

"Drunk or sober, there is no better man to have behind the wheel of a boat," Nonna Maria said.

"It's a police matter, Nonna Maria," Captain Murino said, sorry he'd brought up the subject. "Now, since you didn't come here for my coffee, there must be some other pressing concern for your visit."

"I would like you to look into someone for me," Nonna Maria said. "Someone who has been here less than a month and is set to marry a young girl before the end of the season."

"I'm not a marriage counselor, Nonna Maria," Captain Murino said. "I'm an officer of the law. If this tourist and young girl want to go off and get married, that's their business. It's not a matter for the police."

Nonna Maria leaned her elbows on the captain's desk. "It won't take one of your men long," she said. "These machines you use can find out more in seconds than I could in weeks."

Captain Murino smiled. "I doubt that very much, Nonna Maria," he said. "But, since it's just a simple background check you need, I'll have one of my men look into it. May I have the name of the groom who has aroused your suspicions?"

Nonna Maria nodded. "Bartoli," she said. "Andrea Bartoli."

Captain Murino sat up straight in his leather chair and stared at Nonna Maria. "Andrea Bartoli is here?" he asked. "On Is-chia? Are you certain?"

"I would not be here if I weren't," Nonna Maria said, noting the sudden change of tone in the captain's voice. "Does his name mean something to you?"

Captain Murino stood and turned to stare out at the clear blue waters of the bay, the harbor crowded with boats, the sun gleaming off the waves. "I've never met him," he said in almost a whisper. "I was stationed in Udine soon after I got out of the academy. My youngest sister was to be married, but the station was shorthanded and I couldn't get away to attend the wedding—her wedding to Andrea Bartoli."

Nonna Maria stood and walked over to the captain. "So, this man Bartoli is married," she said to him, gently resting a hand on his right arm. "To your sister. If that's true, then he cannot marry Anna or anyone else."

Captain Murino looked away from the window and at Nonna Maria, his face etched with a sadness she had never before seen in him. "My sister died three months into the marriage," he told her. "It was a quick romance and no one in my family approved, but Clara seemed to walk around in a daze, claiming to be very much in love. Bartoli moved her from Milan to Florence and kept her from having much contact with our family. I had a week's leave due and was planning to go check on my sister with my own eyes. Check on this man Bartoli."

"But you didn't make it in time," Nonna Maria said.

Captain Murino shook his head. "There was a car accident several weeks before I planned to leave, on the autostrada out-side Florence," he said. "It was late at night and Clara died on the scene and was buried the next day. By the time I arrived, Bartoli had left the city. From that day to this, no one in my family ever saw him again."

"Did the police bother to look for him?" Nonna Maria asked.

"They had no reason to look," Captain Murino said. "It was ruled an accident and he was not at fault. My sister was never comfortable behind the wheel of a car, and she took a sharp turn at too high a speed. A heavy rain didn't help matters, and her car skidded and veered into another lane and smashed into the side of a truck. Her car flipped over and caught fire. By the time the fire department got to the scene, it was too late to do her any good."

"But the police must have checked out the car," Nonna Maria said. "Or what was left of it. I know they have to do this whenever an accident such as the one your sister was in happens."

Captain Murino glanced over at Nonna Maria. "How do you know something like that?"

"One of my granddaughters, Rossana, loves watching all the American crime shows on television," Nonna Maria said. "She tells me about some of the things she has learned from watching these programs. She wants to be a lawyer one day, and I guess these shows help her in some way."

"Your granddaughter is correct, at least in that regard," Captain Murino said. "The wreckage of the car was examined but, again, there was nothing they could link to Bartoli."

"Where was he when this accident happened?"

"On a business trip to Pisa," Captain Murino said. "And he had documents to back up his claim. He moved out of the city as soon as the insurance money came through. He left behind a note saying he couldn't face life without his beloved Clara. He was written off by the authorities as a bereaved husband who had suffered a great loss."

"But neither one of us believes that, do we, Captain?" Nonna Maria asked.

"I know I don't," Captain Murino said. "And you already seem convinced. I won't have one of my officers look into the matter. This one I'll deal with myself. As soon as I get back from the port."

"I'll go with you," Nonna Maria said. "See if they managed to find my friend Favorini."

Captain Murino nodded. "I couldn't stop you even if I wanted to."

They made their way slowly out of the station house, through the glass front door and toward the captain's blue squad car. "There's one other thing I should mention about this man who married my sister and is now preparing to marry someone else," he said to Nonna Maria.

Nonna Maria waited as the captain opened the passenger-side door of his car, his right hand still gripping the handle. "Andrea Bartoli is not his real name," Nonna Maria said.

The captain nodded. "How did you already know that?"

"It was more a guess," Nonna Maria said. "But a man who possibly caused the death of one wife and is engaged to another under suspicious circumstances would be a fool to use his real name."

The captain waited as Nonna Maria settled herself in the front seat and looked down at her. "I might as well just give up and give you a carabinieri shield to pin to your dress."

"Don't bother," Nonna Maria said. "I hate jewelry of any kind."

9.

NONNA MARIA SAT silently in the police car as Captain Murino drove down the narrow streets for what would normally be, in the winter months, a five-minute drive to the port. With summer traffic, it would take close to twenty. She stared at the crowds moving slowly on each end of the two-way road, still amazed at how the island had turned so quickly into a major tourist destination.

She understood the appeal and was not, like many of her friends, disturbed by the arrival of the tourists who packed the restaurants, bars, and clubs at night and made it difficult to find an empty spot on many of the island's beautiful beaches. Nonna Maria remembered years when it was not like this, when summers in Ischia meant another season of scraping by, barely making ends meet. Work for many locals was difficult to come by, and the most promising job meant signing up for a six-to-eight-month tour on a cargo ship, away from family and friends.

Nonna Maria always felt outsiders would one day recognize the beauty of Ischia, beyond the healing thermal waters of Poseidon and the mud baths that were said to cure ailments such as back pain and arthritis. She just never imagined they would show up in numbers this large and from places in the world she had barely heard of, let alone visited.

Nonna Maria would often venture outside the port area. On occasion she would head to Ischia Ponte, the next neighborhood over, and walk the streets of her childhood, stare out at the massive Castello Aragonese, stepping on the same black stones that she and her mother once had crossed together. But, for the most part, Nonna Maria lived, as many her age do, with her memories.

She was not a religious woman and didn't attend Sunday services, but she did love to visit the Church of Santa Maria del Soccorso in the borough of Forio. It was a beautiful white stucco church, with a terrace that looked out over the sea. She thought it was the most peaceful place in the world. "If I ever find the need to pray," she once told a friend, "I go to the Church of Santa Maria. I don't need a priest or anyone else to tell me what I should pray for and to whom I should pray and when. That's no one else's business. Only mine."

In the quieter months of the off-season, Nonna Maria would take one of the boats out to the hamlet of Sant'Angelo, a seafront community made up of hundreds of small, clustered multicolored homes. Until 1948 and the construction of a road linking it to the mainland, the only way a visitor could reach Sant'Angelo was by mule train or by walking over from the Maronti beach, long thought to be the island's most coveted spot. Nonna Maria had many friends in the area and remembered visiting the hamlet many times as a child when she would accompany her father on his fishing boat, stopping to drop off his fresh catch to sell to the locals. These days, she would sit with them and enjoy hearing how their summer rentals had fared, who had the best tenants and who the worst.

Sant'Angelo was in the borough of Serrara Fontana, and while there she would be driven near the top of Mount Epomeo, the long-dormant volcano, to visit the vineyards of the D'Ambra family, which dotted the hillsides and slopes of the mountain. The D'Ambras were the largest and best winemakers in Ischia and had been harvesting the land since Nonna Maria was a child. She considered the D'Ambras family and they treated her as one of their own, comfortable in one another's company. After her journey through the vineyards, Nonna Maria would visit with them, have a glass of their latest vintage, and sit across from the heir to the family winery, the youngest daughter of the owner, Sara, and listen to her latest travel adventures visiting wine areas around the world. Nonna Maria marveled at all the wines there were to drink in so many different countries, from South Africa to South America to the United States. Sara was in her early thirties, with dark olive skin warmed by the sun, short hair, charcoal eyes, and an easy smile. She was curious about all things having to do with wine and was determined, through travel and study, to make her family vineyard the best in Southern Italy.

"Does the wine from all these countries taste the same as the wines your family makes?" Nonna Maria had asked on her last visit.

"Each place is different," Sara said. "Some are richer, thicker, much like our Super Tuscans from the North. Others are sweeter, not as heavy as some of the wines from France or Spain."

Nonna Maria smiled. "It's good you get to see all these places and learn their ways," she said. "And I get to see them, as well, through your eyes. But for me, there will only be one wine to drink, and it's made here, by your family."

The wine Nonna Maria had in her kitchen was shipped to her each month by the D'Ambra family and had been for decades. In truth, in her entire life, Nonna Maria had never sampled any other wine.

"A wine you know and trust is like an old friend," Nonna Maria said to Sara. "You can always count on it to be true to you. It will never betray you or let you down. A new wine is much like a new friend: It takes time to develop that trust, that belief that it will never make you regret your choice. And sometimes, not always, that new friend will let you down. Old friends never do."

10.

THE PORT WAS as crowded as Nonna Maria had ever seen it. Police cars were parked at forty-five-degree angles, some with their doors still open. There were at least a dozen carabinieri walking along the edges of the dock; others were circling the area in high-speed motorboats. A handful of boats, filled with Coast Guard scuba teams, were rushing back into the mouth of the harbor. Tourists and locals stood behind yellow police lines, trying to determine if the rumors they had heard were indeed true.

A man was missing and presumed dead, swallowed up sometime during the night by the cold waters of an angry sea.

Nonna Maria stood off to the side, under the awning of Ristorante Alberto, next to crates filled with fresh fish and vegetables brought in earlier in the day, packed in ice and resting in front of the outside tables. She watched as Captain Murino huddled with a number of his officers, listened to their reports, and issued a new array of orders. The men left his side and she watched Captain Murino gaze out at the sea for several moments before he turned, caught her eye, and headed in her direction.

"No signs of a body as yet," Captain Murino told Nonna Maria, standing next to her, his back against the blue iron railing of the empty restaurant. "But I can't imagine anyone, especially a man his age, surviving for very long in the cold waters, especially with such strong currents."

Nonna Maria nodded. "Pasquale liked nothing better than to be on a boat out at sea," she said. "He gave his life to the water. For years, he worked alongside his father, making his living catching and selling fish off their boat. They would leave the port in the middle of the night and return hours later to sell their catch. Then, when the tourists began to come here by the thousands, he left the fish behind and turned to doing tours. It didn't matter what he did, so long as he was out on the water in that boat."

"One of my men tells me he doesn't even have a license to take the boat out," Captain Murino said.

Nonna Maria smiled. "He didn't need a piece of paper to tell him how to pilot a boat," she said. "Pasquale was not one to follow rules."

"Believe me," Captain Murino said, "it has not gone unnoticed."

"Hard to believe a man who knew every inch of that boat and who had crossed the sea, calm or angry, thousands of times could just fall overboard," Nonna Maria said.

"As has been said, he liked his wine," Captain Murino said. "Maybe, on this one night, he had more than he should have had."

"Is that what the first mate tells you?" Nonna Maria asked.

"The first mate hasn't told me anything yet," Captain Murino said. "My men are bringing him to the station house. He'll be questioned there."

"Is he a suspect?" Nonna Maria asked.

"As of now he's a witness," Captain Murino said. "And if the story he tells us holds up, then that's all he will be. But he was the only one on the boat, which, to my mind at least, leaves his complete innocence in doubt."

Nonna Maria moved away from the restaurant and turned to face the captain. "He will tell you his side of the story," she said to him, "and it will be the only side you'll probably get to hear. Unless a miracle occurs, the other side is buried deep under the sea."

"Pasquale's daughters had no interest in taking over the boat from their father when he retired or died," Captain Murino said. "In all probability the boat would have gone to the first mate, with the profits split with Pasquale's widow."

"That's what's been said and that's what I've heard," Nonna Maria said.

"To some, that would be enough to kill for. If Pasquale has been swallowed by the sea, he can't tell us otherwise," Captain Murino said. "And as sad as it is to say, Nonna Maria, the dead can't talk."

Nonna Maria smiled. "On this island, Captain Murino, *everyone* talks," she said. "Even the dead."

11.

THERE WAS A time, decades in the past, when Nonna Maria's daily concerns were limited to caring for her family and managing a small grocery store she and her husband, Gabriel, owned. But even when she was a teenager, growing up in the poorest section of Ischia Ponte, neighbors and friends sought out her advice and looked to her for help.

"She never asked personal questions," her childhood friend, Augusta Mazzoni, used to tell anyone within earshot. "And it was partly for that reason people sought her out. She was so much wiser than her years. You could trust her to respect your wishes and not pass on what she heard from you."

Maria married young, still in her late teens, and had her first child a month before she turned twenty. She was, by all accounts, a beautiful woman—slender, with piercing dark eyes, long dark hair, and a pleasant smile. She doted on her children and adored her husband. "They were in love from the first day, the first moment, they put eyes on each other," Augusta said. "They were the couple every married couple on the island wanted to be like. Believe me, a love and a friendship like they

45

had is not something that is found every day. They were two of the lucky ones."

Maria and Gabriel bought a two-story stone house in the port area, close to one of the many public beaches, and there they raised their seven children. During the island's difficult years, before it was discovered by summer tourists, she and her husband did what they could to help those who were in dire straits. They donated clothes, shipped fresh fruit and vegetables, and distributed goat's milk and cheese from the flock Gabriel maintained on the family property.

The first neighborhood disagreement Maria helped to solve involved a dispute over a newborn infant and two men who claimed to be the child's father—the mother's husband and her lover. This was years before DNA testing was the norm to solve such disputes, and besides, the people of Ischia are suspicious by nature and would not have trusted the results of a test shown to them by a doctor from a lab in Naples.

The trio—husband, wife, lover—sought out Maria to ask her advice. Maria, then in her late thirties, asked to speak to the mother alone. "I want you to talk to your husband and this other man separately," she told her, as they walked up the steep hill to Saint Peter's Church. "Tell them the child is sick and will need a great deal of care and expense before he gets well."

"But my baby is fine," the mother said. "Has been since the day he was born."

Maria nodded. "I know he is," she said. "But one of these men is not the father of your child. And that one might not be so willing to part with money for a child he believes is not his to begin with."

"I've made a mess of my life," the woman said, not bothering to hide her sorrow and the tears that flowed down the sides of her face. "I was angry at my husband for the silliest reasons, and that led me to betray him in a way I never imagined I would."

"Most arguments between a husband and wife are over the most minor issues," Maria said. "But it is not too late to put your life back on the right path and give your child the parents, *both* parents, he deserves."

Three days later, the woman appeared at Maria's front door, her baby in her arms and a smile spread wide across her face. Maria welcomed her inside, rested a cup of coffee in front of the woman, and took the baby from her and held him close. "Your husband has forgiven you," Maria said, smiling down at the baby in her arms. "And your lover is gone from your life."

The woman nodded, still holding the smile. "I did as you asked, Maria," she said. "I spoke to each one alone and told them the baby was ill and would need lots of care and many trips to see specialists in Naples."

"And their reaction?"

"My husband did not hesitate for one moment," the woman said. "He reached for me and held me in his arms. He told me whatever the child needed, no matter how much the cost, he would make sure he would be taken care of. He would work a second, even a third job if necessary. He would do all he could for his son."

"And how did the other man deal with the news?" Maria asked.

"He told me he needed to be sure the baby was his before

he laid out one single lira to care for him," the woman said. "He became angry and raised his voice, telling me this is not what he wanted out of our relationship. He never wanted a family and the expense that came with it. He told me it was over between us and we should never see each other again."

"And he was leaving the island and never coming back," Maria said.

"Yes," the woman said, not bothering to hide the surprise in her voice. "How did you know?"

"Because that's what men like him do," Maria said. "This child now has his family—you and your husband will raise him as your own."

"But, Maria, I still don't know for certain who the real father is," the woman said.

"Yes, you do," Maria said. "You need no more proof than the answers you received from your husband and this other man. No father, married to you or not, would turn his back on his own child. The one who stays and chooses to carry the burden is the baby's real father."

12.

AS WITH ANY great detective, Nonna Maria had accumulated across the years a wide array of trusted sources and confidants, men and women she had known for years and who could come to her aid whenever she needed information or proof. Many of her contacts worked behind the counters of the shops that lined each of the main thoroughfares of the five boroughs; a few were medical personnel who tended to the elderly and the infirm; there were magistrates and lawyers mingled in with pharmacists along with the one dentist on the island.

Nonna Maria knew all the sanitation workers, men who swept the streets and emptied the garbage bins in the early hours of the morning, regardless of season, always with an eye on those out much later than they should be. She was friendly with all the hotel employees, from the concierge of the five-star hotels to the cleaning crews at the smallest bed-and-breakfasts. She was known by every fish peddler and fruit seller on the island and counted among her many friends the plumbers, carpenters, and electricians who helped build the new condos that seemed to crop up each year and tended to the many old houses that were always in need of repair.

Nonna Maria knew them all and could always count on their help. But in her mind, she had no greater source of information than Pepe the Painter. He was Dr. Watson to her Sherlock Holmes. From his perch, painting watercolors on Corso Vittoria Colonna, in front of the Villa Angela, he was able to know, see, and hear anything worth knowing, seeing, or hearing, both good and bad, on the island of Ischia. He set up his easels and color paintings early in the morning, just around sunup, and stayed until the early hours of the next day. He left his post only to buy a panino for lunch and some iced coffee and cigarettes from La Dolce Sosta, a few meters from his station. His finished paintings were lined up against the stone wall of the villa and spread out on a long white table along the very same wall. He charged fifty euros for the smaller paintings and seventy-five to one hundred for the large ones.

On his best days, Pepe the Painter earned three hundred euros for his work. And since this summer was proving to be one of Ischia's best seasons, he was expecting to sell even more of his paintings and enjoy a most comfortable winter.

Nonna Maria walked along the length of the white table, admiring Pepe the Painter's work. Most of the drawings were full-color renditions of the Castello Aragonese or of the various churches of the island. On occasion, he would sketch an image of a woman, sometimes young, occasionally middle-aged, often elderly—but always the same woman. These she knew to be paintings of Pepe's late wife, Lucia, who died a year after Nonna Maria's husband, from the same type of cancer that took his life. It was soon after her death that Pepe took up the work that occupied his days and nights, staying in his large apartment in the borough of Barano just long enough to catch a few hours of restless sleep and gather up some fresh paint, brushes, and mats for his work.

Pepe was a burly man in his mid-fifties, with a thick crop of white hair that he kept long, covering both his ears and the nape of his neck. Despite his chosen profession, he was always neatly dressed, usually in a white cotton shirt with the long sleeves rolled to the center of his arms, khakis that were neatly ironed, and leather open-toed sandals handmade by his brother-in-law, Roberto, in his shop in Barano.

"The painting on the far right would be perfect in your dining room," Pepe said, glancing up and smiling when he saw Nonna Maria. "And I'll sell it to you at a loss. Just knowing it's hanging in your home is all the profit I need."

"Save your energy for the tourists," Nonna Maria said, glancing at the painting on a far corner of the table. "If I want to see the Castello, I can walk to it. I don't need it hanging on my wall."

"If all my customers were like you, I would starve," Pepe said. "But, with good fortune, they're not."

"I'm not here to buy anything," Nonna Maria said, "but I didn't come empty-handed."

She reached into the large black tote bag she often carried with her and pulled out a package wrapped in white butcher paper. "Made you a tomato, basil, and red onion panino," she said. "All grown in my garden."

Pepe the Painter rested his brush against his easel and walked toward Nonna Maria. He wrapped his arms around her and gave her a tight hug. "Did you also put in some of those hot peppers you grow?" he asked. "And that olive oil you get from your niece in Salerno?"

"And some oregano from my daughter Francesca's garden," Nonna Maria said. "The bread is from Don Pietro's ovens, and the slices of cheese are from my neighbor."

"Which neighbor?" Pepe asked, slowly unwrapping the large sandwich. "The one who sings all the time or the one with the one eye?"

"The one you like," Nonna Maria said. "The singer."

"Brava," Pepe said. "She has a voice handed to her by the angels above themselves."

"You say that because you don't have to listen to her day and night," Nonna Maria said. "Even the angels need a break from hearing her sing."

Pepe pulled a folded wooden chair from behind his easel, opened it, and placed it in front of Nonna Maria. "Please, sit with me while I enjoy the special treat you brought. And before we talk about the real reason for your visit, may I ask if you also brought some wine for me to drink with this delicious panino?"

Nonna Maria reached into her tote bag and brought out a corked bottle of white and an empty glass. "It can't be called a meal without wine," she said.

"Bravissima, Nonna Maria," Pepe the Painter said, taking a huge bite from the sandwich, watching as she poured him a full glass of wine and rested it along with the bottle by his feet. "Now, what is it you need from me?"

"Everything you know or have heard about Giovanni Buon-opana," Nonna Maria said.

Pepe the Painter nodded as he chewed his food. "The young man who was with poor Pasquale when he fell into the sea?" he asked.

"Yes," Nonna Maria said. "That Giovanni Buonopana."

13.

NONNA MARIA WALKED slowly back to her house, going down the sloping hill, easing her way past the tourists crowding into restaurants and shops and locals out for a late-evening stroll. She nodded to several familiar faces as she walked but seemed more focused on a tall, middle-aged man in a white straw hat who was walking several feet behind her, doing his utmost to appear inconspicuous.

Nonna Maria stopped and greeted one of the young staff members of Naturischia, a shop that sold varieties of local wines, lotions and cups, magnets and aprons with photos of the island on them. The shop had been a staple of the port area since her children were young, and she had known the original owners since she herself was a child.

"Buona sera, Nonna Maria," the young woman, Gabriella, said. She was standing in the entrance to the shop, hoping to catch a cool breeze after a long day working behind the register. "I don't know about you, but I can't wait for Sunday to arrive. With this heat, there's no better place to be than at the beach, in cool water up to my neck."

Nonna Maria smiled at the girl. She was wearing a short-sleeved white blouse and a tight pair of stone-washed jeans and red sandals. She had long dark hair held in the back by two large brown clips and was ready for the end of her day.

"Your workload will ease when Assunta returns from her trip to Florence," Nonna Maria said. "She's the oldest, and the oldest always carries the heaviest burden. It was true for my children and it is true for you and your sister."

"But who knows when she'll return, Nonna Maria," Gabriella said. "I ask my mother and father all the time and I get the same answer. 'Any day now,' and, to me, that's no answer at all."

"It's her first time in a big city," Nonna Maria said. "And there's so much to see in Florence. It's the home of our greatest artists and thinkers. You'll go there one day and you'll see for yourself."

"You've been there?"

Nonna Maria shook her head. "But you know how it is," she said. "People talk and sometimes they talk about Florence. And sometimes I listen to the talk."

Nonna Maria saw a basket to Gabriella's right and moved into the shop to get a closer look. As she did, she took a quick glance to her right and spotted the man in the white straw hat across the way, at a bar, drinking a beer from a frosted glass.

"Take one if you like," Gabriella said. "They're homemade lemon candies. My mama makes them from the lemons in our garden."

"And if they're from Nunzia's garden, they must be excellent," Nonna Maria said. "I'll take a kilo. But they're not for me. For my grandchildren. The teeth I have left I don't plan to lose."

Gabriella went into the store and came out with a white

paper bag and filled it with the cellophane-wrapped candies. She weighed the bag on a small scale to her right and handed it to Nonna Maria. "You don't owe me money," she said to Nonna Maria. "You have a twenty-euro credit from the last time you shopped here, remember? It was the day I only had large bills in the register and you told me not to worry, you'd be back."

"And I'll be back again," Nonna Maria said. "As long as I have grandchildren, I will always be in need of candy."

Nonna Maria turned to leave, looked across the way at the man in the straw hat, and glanced over at Gabriella. "Do you have a way to get in touch with Don Marco?" she asked.

"Yes," Gabriella said, smiling. "I have his cell number and can call him if you like. But it seems a bit late for him to hear your confession, Nonna Maria."

"I haven't been to confession since I was about your age," Nonna Maria said, returning the smile. "If Don Marco were to hear mine now, we would be there until the sun came up. Call him for me, anyway. Tell him I'm heading home and he should come meet me from the back of the church. The same way he used when he came to meet my older grandsons on their way to the beach. But he should let me pass first and wait for a minute or two. Until he hears footsteps behind me. Then he should come out."

Gabriella quickly lost the smile and pulled a cell phone out of the rear pocket of her jeans. "Are you in trouble, Nonna Maria?" she asked, reaching out a hand for the older woman.

Nonna Maria patted the young girl's face and gently rubbed her arm. "Not to worry," she said. "If there is trouble, it's the kind an old woman like me and a young priest like Don Marco have seen before."

14.

ANNA HELD ON to an aluminum post as the front of the fast-moving motorboat bobbed and weaved against the force of a rapid tide. The young man manning the wheel turned to her and gave her a reassuring smile. "The water will calm down soon as we make the turn past the big rocks up ahead," he said. "From then on, it will be as if you were an infant being rocked in a cradle."

The young man's name was Luca Lo Manto and he had owned the twenty-foot boat for three years now, working to pay off the thirty thousand euros he spent to buy it with the four hundred fifty euros he earned per day, taking tourists on excursions around the island and as far as the nearby islands of Capri and Procida. The boat fit as many as eight, though he seldom booked more than four at a time. He would make several stops during the eight-hour day, three to allow his passengers to swim in the calm waters of a hidden bay and once to take them for a long lunch in a restaurant that could only be reached by water. "It's the best food on the island," he would tell them in any one of the four languages he spoke, "and no one even knows where it is. Except for me."

Luca was twenty-six, thin, with thick dark hair and a beard to match. His skin was the color of tea with milk, warmed by the many days spent on open waters, and he loved taking his boat out during the summer months. When the season ended, Luca would sign up for work on a cargo ship, leaving in early November and returning to his beloved island at the end of March, his pockets crammed with the six thousand euros a month he had earned traveling through treacherous waters and dropping off cargo to ports he had previously only read about in adventure magazines as a boy.

Luca was Nonna Maria's oldest grandson. So when she asked him to take Anna on his boat for several days and keep her away from prying eyes, he didn't hesitate. He packed enough food and water and wine to keep them fed for a week and knew that if he needed to stay out longer, he could count on the owner of the hidden restaurant to restock his provisions. He didn't ask who Anna was hiding from, figuring if she wanted to confide in him, she would, and if she didn't, that would be fine, as well. All he knew on this his first full day with the nervous young woman was that his Nonna needed her kept out of sight.

"Do you want to take the wheel?" Luca asked Anna. "Drive the boat for a while?"

Anna seemed surprised by the request. "I've never driven a boat before," she said, not bothering to hide her smile, her cheeks quickly turning apple red. "I wouldn't know how."

"You're from Ischia, am I right?" Luca asked.

Anna nodded.

"Everyone from Ischia knows how to drive a boat," Luca said. "This will just be your first time. Keep both hands on the wheel and follow the flow of the water. If you need any help, I'll be right here next to you."

They exchanged places and Anna took control of the wheel. "Keep the boat out to the left," Luca told her. "You never want to get too close to the rock side. Unless you want to drop anchor and go for a swim."

The wind picked up, and Anna, after an initial bout of nerves, began to feel comfortable, navigating the boat between the hard slaps of the swells and the calm comfort of the blue-green waters.

"How am I doing?" she asked Luca.

"You handle the wheel like a born sailor," Luca said. "And believe me, I don't say that to every passenger who I've had behind the wheel. Some of them pull and turn it in all directions—next thing I know we're heading straight for the cliffs. It's all I can do to get them away from the wheel."

Anna pointed to the large cooler filled with ice, prosecco, white wine, and beer. "It might be because they've had more than their share to drink before they take the wheel," she said.

Luca smiled. "Eight hours is a long time for many of them to be out on the water," he said. "They're not used to it. The drink relaxes them, and then, after a long lunch and even more drinking, they're ready for a nap. It makes the trip go faster. For them and for me."

"I haven't thanked you for letting me stay on your boat," she said. "And you haven't asked why."

"It's not for me to ask," Luca said, staring at the sparkling waters, his face up toward the warm sun. "And you don't need to thank me. I would do anything Nonna asked me to do."

"I'm supposed to marry a man I'm not in love with," Anna said, relieved to be talking about it. "And I went to your Nonna to see if she could be of help."

"Why not just break off the engagement?" Luca asked. "Cancel the wedding. You wouldn't be the first bride to change her mind about a wedding. It's done all the time."

Anna stayed silent for a moment before answering. "Nonna Maria thinks he's a dangerous man," she said, "and is afraid of what he might do if I cancel the wedding. Not just to me but to my family. She wants me out of his sight until she can figure out the best way to free me from the situation."

"What makes her think that?" Luca asked. "Did he threaten you?"

Anna shook her head. "Like I told Nonna Maria, I don't remember much of what happened these past few weeks. But as each day passes, some moments become clearer to me."

"Moments that frightened you," Luca said.

Anna nodded. "One night, soon after we met, we were having dinner and his cell phone rang," she said. "He glanced at the number and grew agitated. He excused himself from the table and took the call in a corner of the room. When he returned, he was angry and had a strange look in his eyes."

"Did you say anything to him?"

"I wondered what was wrong and asked if there was anything I could do to help," Anna said. "He stared at me for the longest time and then drank a full glass of wine. Then he leaned closer to me and said there was something I could do and that was to not be like the last woman he married. To not be the kind of wife who haunts a man. Even from the grave."

Luca stared at Anna for a few moments, and then his hand reached out and grabbed a cell phone resting on a thin shelf just below the boat's instrument panel. "Did you mention this to Nonna?" he asked. He was scanning through his phone, found a number and pressed the dial button.

"Yes," Anna said. "We were walking to your boat when I told her the story. That gave her one more reason to keep me out of sight. She believes this is about more than just a wedding. That Bartoli might have something sinister planned, and she wants him stopped before it can get to that point. She said she needs my help as much as I need hers."

Luca looked at her and nodded, the phone against his ear, his back to the wind, allowing him to hear better once his call went through.

"Who are you calling?" Anna asked, her voice now a mixture of fear and tangled nerves.

"A friend," Luca said.

15.

NONNA MARIA WALKED slowly down the sloping street, careful not to slide on the damp cobblestones. She walked as close to the rear entrance of the church as she could, the street ahead shrouded in darkness, the noise of the tourist-jammed Corso behind her now a blur of white noise. She wore her usual pair of black leather sandals and, with her widow's black blouse and long skirt, would be all but invisible to anyone around her if not for her thick strands of white hair. She chewed on one of the lemon-flavored candies she had bought from Gabriella, the rest filling a side pocket of her skirt.

She felt the man in the straw hat's presence before she heard him, walking in a steady stride behind her, closing in, a stealth figure moving in measured silence. Nonna Maria stopped as soon as she felt the man's hard grip on her right shoulder. She turned to face him, standing firm, her eyes looking up at the tall, thin man.

"I hear you've been asking about me," he said to her in a low voice. "And now my bride is missing and I have a strong feeling you know where she went. Am I right, old woman?"

"I don't like to talk much," Nonna Maria said. "And I like to talk even less to someone I don't know. Especially if that someone has taken a hand to me."

The man smiled and released his grip. "I like that you're not afraid," he said. "I've heard that about you. But you should be. I'm not a man you want to be on the wrong side of. That's not a safe place for anyone."

"Especially a woman," Nonna Maria said.

"Where is she?" he asked. "Tell me where Anna is. If you do, there's a chance this night won't end as bad as it might for you."

Nonna Maria glanced up at the white stone walls of Saint Peter's and shrugged. "Lucky for me, then, that we're close to a church," she said. "They won't have to go out of their way for my funeral mass."

"A church, I might add, that Nonna Maria has not once attended in the three years I've been the parish priest."

The thin man in the straw hat turned and found himself facing a young man in dark slacks and a white T-shirt. Even in the shrouded darkness, the thin man could tell he was strong, his biceps bulging and his hands curled into fists. His voice was calm, but his body was tense and seemed primed to attack.

"What do you want with Nonna Maria?" the young man asked.

"This doesn't concern you," the thin man said. "Go on your way and leave the matter to the two of us."

"Despite her poor attendance record, Nonna Maria belongs to my parish," the young man said. "And what kind of priest would I be if I let someone bring her harm?"

"Don't think if you come to my rescue, you'll see me in

church on Sunday, Don Marco," Nonna Maria said. "What happens tonight changes nothing."

Don Marco smiled. "But I will come by your house after high mass," he said. "And there we'll pray together before we eat your delicious pasta and fresh tomatoes and basil and drink chilled white wine with peaches."

Nonna Maria smiled at the young priest. "That's *my* idea of a perfect church," she said.

Don Marco turned to face the thin man, his smile gone, his voice taking on a harder tone. "If you so much as push her, I swear to my God, I will be giving you last rites before the sun rises," he said.

The thin man glared at Don Marco and then smiled. "I don't expect I'll get any trouble from you," he said. "It's not in a priest's nature to get violent. And it's not like you can arrest me. So there's really nothing you can do, other than pray for me."

"But I can arrest you, Bartoli," Captain Murino said. "Not even Don Marco's prayers can prevent that."

He was standing behind Bartoli. Murino was out of uniform, dressed in light-colored jeans and a loose-fitting blue polo shirt.

"A citizen's arrest?" Bartoli asked.

Captain Murino lifted the right side of the polo shirt to reveal his carabinieri shield and shook his head. "A citizen would bring you to me. But since I'm already here, that's a step we can skip."

Bartoli stepped away from Nonna Maria and Don Marco and moved closer to the captain. "If you were to arrest me," he said, "what would the charge be?"

"He was about to harm Nonna Maria," Don Marco said. "He stopped just as I arrived."

"And we have a witness," Captain Murino said. "And not just any witness but a priest. Even the best lawyer your money can buy would have a tough time winning that case, Bartoli."

"How do you know my name?" Bartoli asked.

"I know quite a bit about you," Captain Murino said. "Even your real name. What I don't know is why you were confronting Nonna Maria. Your usual targets are younger women. From financially sound families and with life-insurance policies that can easily be transferred to your name."

"It's the old woman you should be looking at," Bartoli said. "Not me. She has taken my fiancée away. Possibly done her harm. My Anna is missing."

"Is that true, Nonna Maria?" Captain Murino asked. "You have taken away his fiancée?"

Nonna Maria shook her head. "The young girl is to be married next week," she said. "She's nervous, as most young brides are. She needed a few days to herself. There's nothing more sinister to it than that."

"It's a tradition here on Ischia," Don Marco said. "A bride spends the last few days prior to the ceremony with friends and family and away from her future husband."

"For what purpose?" Bartoli asked.

"When she's married, she will no longer be the center of their world," Don Marco said. "She will be part of her new husband's world. She'll still be a daughter and friend, but she will also be a man's wife. The time alone is a time of thanks and reflection and preparing for her new life."

"It's a foolish tradition," Bartoli said. "We don't allow for such nonsense in the North."

"It might have saved a woman's life if they did," Captain Murino said. "A woman who made the mistake of marrying you. A woman who died because of you, Bartoli."

Bartoli stepped closer to the captain, their faces inches apart. "Don't you dare speak to me about my wife," he said, his voice barely above a whisper. "You don't know anything about her."

"I know everything about her, Bartoli," Captain Murino said. "Clara was my sister. And I know that it was you who caused her death. I won't bring you in for what occurred here tonight. Even with Don Marco as a witness, you'll walk away with nothing stronger than a warning. But I will get you on a much bigger charge. I will get you for killing my sister."

Bartoli stayed silent for a moment and then spoke in a calm, relaxed manner. "Clara's death was declared an accident," he said. "A tragic accident in which I played no part."

Captain Murino stared at Bartoli and then stepped away from him. "Be on your way," he said. "We'll meet again soon enough. The next time, however, will not end with you walking away a free man. That I promise you."

Bartoli nodded at Don Marco and then turned to Nonna Maria. "I hope I didn't frighten you, widow," he said to her. "I acted only out of concern for my Anna."

"Men like you never frighten me," Nonna Maria said.

She stood between Captain Murino and Don Marco and watched as Bartoli made his way back up the hill and disappeared into the thick throng of tourists lining the Corso.

16.

THE NEXT MORNING, Captain Murino sat across from Nonna Maria, sipping a cup of her strong espresso. He waited as her nephew monitored her blood pressure. His name was Agostino and he was the premier physician on the island. Fresh out of medical school, Agostino Mattera had graduated at the top of his class and could have had his pick of any medical facility in Northern Italy. Hospitals from Bologna to Milan to Florence attempted to recruit him. But Agostino had his mind made up even before he walked through the doors of the imposing medical school building in Naples to begin his studies. He wanted to be an island doctor, returning to Ischia to care for the people he had known since he was a child, the people he loved and respected.

People in need of a doctor with his immense talents.

Agostino glanced over at Captain Murino and nodded at the coffee. "I see you share the same habits as my aunt," he said in a voice as soft as an afternoon breeze. "It's no wonder you two are such good friends."

Agostino always spoke in calm tones, never one to raise his voice. He was short, with an easy smile and a gentle way about him that relaxed even the most nervous of patients. His thick hair was turning from light brown to gray, and his eyes were the color of a starless sky. He had married a woman he met in medical school, and together they raised a family that had grown to three children and shared a practice, working out of a small villa between the port and Ischia Ponte. They lived in the villa next door to their medical studio.

Captain Murino held the cup close to his lips. "It's only my second cup of the morning, Doctor," he said, somewhat defensively. "I seldom, if ever, have more than three in one day."

Agostino looked at his aunt and smiled. "One cup of my aunt's coffee equals three cups of any coffee you will find in any café on the island," he said. "It not only wakes up your heart, it kicks up your blood pressure. Why do you think I'm here every week to check on her?"

"To keep your wife happy with the jars of fresh tomato sauce you take home to her," Nonna Maria said.

Agostino looked at the captain. "She knows me too well," he said. "She's a magician in the kitchen, as anyone who has sat at her table will tell you. But I'm sure you're not here this morning to share recipes with my aunt. I'm just about done with my exam, and then I'll leave you two to whatever business it is you need to discuss."

"No need to rush, Doctor," Captain Murino said. "What I have to say will be known soon enough from here to the top of Mount Epomeo. Good news travels at a slow pace in Ischia, but bad news moves faster than the rapido from Naples to Florence."

"You found Pasquale's body," Nonna Maria said, not bothering to hide the sadness she felt.

"I'm afraid so," Captain Murino said. "Coast Guard divers

found him washed ashore on one of the small beaches by the rocks near Casamicciola."

"And you're assuming he drowned?"

"An autopsy will be done later today," Captain Murino said. "But a preliminary examination of the body showed no external wounds, other than a large bump on the side of his head. And that could have happened when he fell overboard night before last."

"*If* he fell overboard," Nonna Maria said.

"He was drinking heavily that night," Captain Murino said. "More than his usual share. The first mate, Buonopana, claims Pasquale was so drunk he couldn't even control the wheel. He had steered far off course."

"And where was Buonopana when Pasquale fell overboard?" Nonna Maria asked.

"He claims he was asleep in one of the bunks belowdeck," Captain Murino said.

"And yet, as drunk as he claims his captain was, Buonopana had no problem leaving him behind the wheel while he slept," Nonna Maria said.

"Buonopana was the only one on that boat other than Pasquale, so far as we know," Captain Murino said. "While it does not as yet make him a suspect, it does make him a person of interest. Perhaps he had grown tired of waiting for Pasquale to retire."

"The boat would be his eventually, that much is known to anyone working at the port," Nonna Maria said.

"The boy is young and inexperienced," Captain Murino said. "And Pasquale was not an easy man to work for. Drunk or sober, he expected his orders to be followed."

"Did Buonopana hear Pasquale fall into the water?" Nonna Maria asked.

"The water was choppy, and the boat rocked back and forth," he said. "The waves were slapping onto the front of the boat. With all that activity, it would be difficult to hear someone going over the side."

"But not too difficult to sleep," Nonna Maria said. "Even with a dog barking."

"What dog?" Captain Murino asked. "Buonopana told us there was no one on the boat other than him and Pasquale."

"Pasquale never went anywhere without Pippo," Nonna Maria said. "He loved that dog like a son. And when Pasquale went out on the boat, Pippo was always by his side. Always."

"It doesn't sound to me like my aunt believes the version this young man told you," Agostino said to Captain Murino.

Captain Murino downed the last of his coffee and nodded. "Nor do I," he said. "It's too neat. But we have no other witnesses and Pasquale was most likely drunk, as the autopsy report no doubt will confirm."

"And what about Pippo?" Nonna Maria asked.

"It's possible the dog jumped into the water with his master," Captain Murino said. "Especially if he was as close to Pasquale as you say. He could have drowned along with the old man. A rough sea can swallow two as easily as it can swallow one."

"And Buonopana gets the boat," Nonna Maria said.

Captain Murino nodded. "As you noted, Buonopana claims it was promised to him when Pasquale retired. But that will need to wait until the magistrate reads the will, assuming he left one."

"There's still time, then," Nonna Maria said.

"Time for what?" Captain Murino said.

"For us to find a witness," Nonna Maria said. "And to prove for certain that Pasquale's death was not an accident but a murder."

Nonna Maria pushed her chair back and began to walk toward the front door of her home. Agostino stood by the entrance and held up one hand. "Before you head out, Sherlock Holmes, you need to take one of the pills I've left for you on the table."

She walked back to the table, poured herself a small glass of wine from the bottle of white resting next to a bowl of fresh fruit. She opened the plastic bottle of pills and took one out. She swallowed the pill and drank the wine.

"When will the autopsy report be ready?" she asked Captain Murino.

"Maybe tomorrow," Captain Murino said. "More likely the day after. But it will only tell us what we already know, Nonna Maria. Pasquale was drunk, lost his balance when one of the waves hit against the side of his boat, and he fell overboard, possibly banging his head before he crashed into the water."

"Do you believe that's what happened?" Nonna Maria asked.

"I believe what the evidence tells me," Captain Murino said. "And, for now at least, that's where it points. But it's a fresh investigation; new evidence might emerge before all is said and done. And that evidence might make us take a harder look at young Buonopana."

"Like a boat on open waters, evidence can change course," Nonna Maria said. "All it takes is one tilt of the wheel."

Captain Murino looked at Nonna Maria and took a deep breath. "I'll have my men check the boat again," he said. "Go through it from top to bottom and see if they find anything that might tilt our wheel in another direction."

Nonna Maria smiled at him and headed toward the door. Agostino reached down and gave her a warm hug. "I'll see you next week," he said. "Keep taking one of those pills every day, and try not to drink too much coffee. As a favor to me."

Nonna Maria nodded and walked out the front door of her two-story home. She stopped at the landing and looked at her nephew. "Agostino?"

Agostino poked his head around a stone wall. "Don't worry," he said. "I won't forget to take the jars of tomato sauce."

"You called me Sherlock Holmes," Nonna Maria said. "Who is that?"

"He's someone who helps those in need," Agostino said. "Much like you do. You're the Sherlock Holmes of Ischia. It's what a number of my patients call you."

"Is he good at what he does?"

"They say he's the best," Agostino said. "But he doesn't work alone. He has a partner."

"And who is that?"

"A doctor," Agostino said. "They work together to help solve the cases they take on."

"I don't need a partner," Nonna Maria said, starting her descent down the stairs. "Especially not a doctor. I like to drink my coffee and my wine in peace."

17.

NONNA MARIA SAT on a small wooden stool as she tightened the fresh bandage she had wrapped around her sister-in-law's leg. Nella Amato was in her mid-seventies and the last remaining sibling of Nonna Maria's late husband, Gabriel. She was wearing a light-blue summer dress and had a thick black cotton sweater draped across her shoulders. She was frail, her voice raspy, and she had trouble seeing out of one eye. She had thick silver hair hanging down the sides of her neck and coming to rest in the center of her back. She had a crooked smile and always had small bottles of pear juice beside her rocking chair.

In the years of Nonna Maria's engagement and then marriage, she and Nella went out of their way to avoid each other. Nella had no use for her sister-in-law, and Nonna Maria did her best to ignore the slights and snide comments Nella aimed at her the times they were forced together. Nella called her vile names and suggested that she was both an unfit wife and ill-suited to be a mother. Nella's hatred toward her sister-in-law ran deep and endured for decades. The pleas of Nonna Maria's husband to bring the vitriol to an end only fell on deaf ears.

"She hates me and I ignore her," Nonna Maria used to tell

her children about her relationship with their aunt. Nella never slighted her nieces and nephews and could be counted on to be overly generous to them, especially during the holidays. She adored her older brother, though she ignored his frequent requests to attempt to get along with Nonna Maria. Across many decades, a cold war settled in between the two women.

Then, ten years ago, Nella, now a widow and without her only child, Marco, by her side, found herself in a dire situation. Her son had died young, not yet twenty years old, his body found in an alley on the outskirts of Naples, a victim of a drug overdose. She had little in the way of money, a bad leg in need of regular medical attention, and was a week away from being evicted from her home due to nonpayment of rent.

Word about her sister-in-law's plight quickly found its way to Nonna Maria. The easy path would have been to turn her back on a woman who had done nothing but belittle her for decades. But that was not the way Nonna Maria chose to live her life.

Instead, within a few days, she found Nella a place to live and had her nephew the doctor call in a specialist to look at Nella's damaged leg and come up with a medical solution that would ease her pain. She also arranged for Nella's groceries to be delivered to her twice a week and made sure she had enough water and wine.

As the years passed, a thaw settled between the once-bitter enemies. They would never be close friends, but they had learned to tolerate each other. One grateful for the care and help she received from a woman who could have easily shunned her. The other happy to be of help to the last of her husband's brothers and sisters.

Nonna Maria stood up from the stool, a plastic wash basin cradled in her hands, half-filled with gray water and blood-soaked bandages. "You need to walk if you want that leg to get better," Nonna Maria said. "Use the cane I bought you and walk around the apartment. Get the blood flowing. It will never heal if you leave it resting on the bench."

"It hurts for me to move it," Nella said. "With or without the cane."

"It's always going to hurt," Nonna Maria said. "But it's going to hurt more if you don't move around. I'll have the doctor come later and take a look at it. But I'm pretty sure he'll tell you the same thing I'm telling you, and that's to move."

Nella watched as Nonna Maria walked to the bathroom and emptied the basin and began to scrub it clean. "People are talking," Nella said, her voice loud enough for Nonna Maria to hear above the running water. "I hear them as they walk past me in the morning. I keep the door open to let the sun warm my leg."

Nonna Maria stepped out of the bathroom, drying her hands on a blue towel. "Not that it matters to me, but what is it these people are saying you think I need to hear?" she asked.

"Mostly about poor Pasquale and his accident," Nella said. "Well, some call it an accident. Others are not so sure."

Nonna Maria stepped in closer to Nella. "Which others?" she asked.

"Piero, Umberto the florist's youngest son, is one," Nella said. "He always stops by to say hello and talk for a time when he's in the area. He and my Marco were always together when they were teenagers. That was before my boy went to Naples and fell into a world he should never have been in."

"What does Piero say about Pasquale's death?"

"He thinks the drugs that killed my Marco have now found their way here, to Ischia," Nella said. "They're coming in from Naples and are sold in the dark of night to anyone who will buy them. It makes sense in a way. All these tourists, pockets filled with money and eager to spend it."

Nonna Maria pulled a wood chair closest to the dining room table and sat down next to Nella. "And what do drugs have to do with Pasquale's death?" she asked.

"Piero says small tour boats are the easiest way for the drugs to be brought into Ischia," Nella said. "The Coast Guard and the carabinieri monitor the large boats and hydrofoils and check the cars that come onto the island by boat."

"But the smaller tour boats don't go as far as Naples," Nonna Maria said. "So they're not watched as closely."

"And they head out late at night, to refuel or for repairs," Nella said. "Out there, they could be met by a boat from Naples and the drugs transferred from one to the other."

Nonna Maria sat in silence for a moment and then shook her head. "Pasquale would never do such a thing," she said. "He would not turn his eye from a case of wine, but never drugs. He was an honest man."

"That is true," Nella said. "*If* he knew what his boat was being used for. By the hour his boat was being taken to Forio for gas or parts, Pasquale was well into his third bottle of wine. I know he never surrendered his wheel when tourists were aboard, but that late at night, with an empty boat and a long ride ahead of him? Why not let the first mate take control?"

"A first mate eager for a boat of his own," Nonna Maria said.

"Or maybe in need of money to pay off a debt. And letting drugs be moved on Pasquale's boat was the fastest way to pay them off."

"I know two things about drugs," Nella said. "They can make a poor man rich in a matter of months, and they kill you years before your time."

"There's a third thing about drugs you should know," Nonna Maria said. "Something we should all know."

"What?" Nella said, wiping tears from her wrinkled face with the curled fingers of a hand whose bones would no longer bend.

"They can lead even the most innocent to make foolish decisions," Nonna Maria said. "Trusting in men they should never trust and whose words they should never believe. Men who put them on a path that only leads to death."

18.

NONNA MARIA WAS sitting on a garden chair on the top deck of the *Princess,* a two-hundred-forty-passenger tour boat that was the largest working on the island. Next to her, both hands on the controls, was the ship's co-owner and captain, Silvio Rumore. He was middle-aged, with long strands of thick blond hair rustling in the wind, his once-muscular frame surrendering to too much wine and pasta. He was shirtless and wore shorts, as was his normal custom, especially when the ship was free of tourists.

Nonna Maria had known Silvio since he was a child and his parents even longer. They were also linked by marriage: One of Silvio's nieces had married one of Nonna Maria's grandsons. Her grandson had died several years back of a heart ailment, leaving behind a widow with two small children. And both sides of the family made sure that all three were cared for and were never at a loss for anything.

Silvio eased the ship out of the port, gliding past motorboats and idle tankers, his maneuvers as slow and gentle as if he were cradling a newborn infant. Most men on the island grew up in one of two ways—on the water, learning about boats at an early age, either through fishing or the tourist trade, or on the road, where cars and motorcycles fed their passion, the men caring for them, maintaining them, and driving them through the winding roads of Ischia until it was second nature.

Silvio glanced down and spotted the large wicker basket Nonna Maria had brought on board with her. "Is what's in there all for you?" he asked, smiling. "Or are you going to share it?"

Nonna Maria lifted the basket and rested it on the top step leading down to the galley and slid open the lid. "None of it is for me," she said. "I packed it all for you. We'll start with coffee and a fresh pastry. But don't have too many, because I made chicken the way you like it for lunch. Along with the stuffed peppers."

Silvio patted his stomach with both hands. "My wife has ordered me to lose weight," he said. "Told me she wants back the tall, handsome man she married, not a fat, old, long-haired man who eats and drinks too much."

"That means she still loves you," Nonna Maria said. "But our clocks don't move backward, only forward, no matter how hard we try to stop them."

Nonna Maria handed Silvio a plastic cup filled with hot espresso and a warm pastry wrapped in foil. He released his grip on the wheel, flipped two buttons on the console, took the coffee and pastry from her, and sat back in his swivel chair. "I've known you for many years, Nonna Maria," he said, sipping the coffee and then biting into the sweet pastry. "And I don't think you prepared a feast for me to consume just to keep me company while I take my ship to Forio and have it serviced. You have questions you want to ask, and for some reason you think I might have the answers."

"You always were the smartest one in your family," Nonna Maria said. "I'm happy to see age has only sharpened your instincts."

"Let me have a second cup of your coffee," Silvio said, handing her the empty plastic cup, "and I'll do my best to answer any questions you ask."

"Would you have let Pasquale pilot the *Princess*?" she asked, pouring out a second cup from a large silver thermos. "Especially these last few years, when he was drinking more?"

Silvio looked out at the calm waters and nodded. "Drunk or sober, Pasquale was the best man I've ever seen behind the wheel of a boat or ship. He could pilot a ship as big as this one or the smallest dinghy and bring it safely into harbor blind and with one hand. He knew these waters better than any man who sailed across them. Even better than my own father, and you know yourself how good he was."

"But you heard how they say he died," Nonna Maria said.

"It doesn't mean I believe it," Silvio said. "He was old, and he was a drunk. And he didn't hide it. But he went out every morning, his boat crammed with as many tourists as he could fit, and he brought them in safe each night. That's all you can ask from any captain."

"So you don't think he fell overboard and hit his head," Nonna Maria said.

"When I first started going out with my father on this boat, he wouldn't drink until all the tourists were safely back on land," Silvio said. "Then, as we headed back to dock for the night—and in those years we couldn't afford to pay the docking fees in the port, so we had to journey back to Forio—my father would open the cooler and take out his wine. And he drank until he was drunk. But if he felt himself getting too drunk, you know what he did then?"

"Tell me," Nonna Maria said.

"He would hand me the wheel, ask me to keep the engine in neutral, strip off his shirt and pants, and jump into the cold water," Silvio said. "He would swim around for maybe ten, fifteen minutes. Then he'd come back on the ship, towel down, put on his clothes, take the wheel, and put the engine in drive. And he was as sober as a young monk. The cold water took away the drunk."

"And Pasquale used to do the same?"

"They all did, Nonna Maria," Silvio said. "It was how they had been taught by their fathers and grandfathers. Let's remember, they didn't lead easy lives. They worked these waters for long hours and sometimes for very little money. The Ischia of my father and of Pasquale was different than the island you see now. Now you can make yourself a rich man working the tourist trade. Back then there were just enough tourists to pay for fuel and food for the family. And they didn't have to buy the wine. That they made themselves."

"I remember both Pasquale and your father and many of the others, during the feast of Saint Anne, decorating their boats and driving them to the castle, to see which one would win for best in show," Nonna Maria said. "The competition between them was strong, but so was the friendship."

"They took their enjoyment where they could find it," Silvio said. "It's very different today. The old men had nothing in front of them but open sea. One of my captains—about thirty, maybe a little older, working on one of my other boats—texts with his girlfriend and watches movies on an iPad when he's taking the tourists out. One time, he got too close to the rocks near Barano and almost ripped the bottom out of the ship. And he was sober."

"Where is Pasquale's boat now?" Nonna Maria asked.

"In dry dock in Forio," Silvio said. "We'll pass it on our way to get my ship serviced."

"How long will it take for them to work on your ship?"

"Two hours, maybe less," Silvio said. "More than enough time for me to enjoy the feast you prepared."

"Are the carabinieri guarding Pasquale's boat?" Nonna Maria asked.

Silvio shook his head. "I don't see why they still would be," he said. "Pasquale's death is being treated as an accident. To this point, no crime has been committed, which means there's no reason to block access to the boat."

"And would you be allowed on board?"

"He was a friend and a fellow captain," Silvio said. "No one would have a problem if I boarded to show my respect."

Nonna Maria smiled. "Will they have a problem with an old widow boarding the ship to do the same?"

Silvio smiled. "I can't imagine why anyone would object," he said.

"Good, then," Nonna Maria said. "Get me on board the boat. Then you take the basket, find a nice table in the shade, and enjoy the meal I prepared. That will give me plenty of time to spend on Pasquale's boat."

"What are you looking for?" Silvio asked.

"I'll know it when I find it," Nonna Maria said.

19.

NONNA MARIA STEPPED onto Pasquale's boat, walking on unsteady legs as small ripples of waves splashed against the sides. She held on to the railings as she made her way from the rear of the boat to the front, eyes searching for any sign of something that shouldn't be there, something that didn't belong. She made her way down to the galley and scanned the shelves and looked over the two small beds, their sheets unfurled, the thin mattresses resting against the chipped wood panels. The small kitchen contained nothing but an espresso pot, some canned goods, and a half-gallon bottle of wine. The space smelled of oil and wet clothes. She accidentally kicked over a garbage bin and was surprised to find it empty. Next to it was a small roll of white plastic liners.

She opened the wood drawer of a cabinet located under one of the bunks. Inside, she found a number of wrinkled sweaters, soiled long-sleeved shirts, and two pairs of pants. She took out the clothes and checked through the pockets. All were empty. She stood and was making her way up the narrow galley steps when she glanced over at a large coffee tin, its label ripped off long ago. She picked up the half-empty tin and flicked off the plastic top. The strong aroma of coffee helped to fend off the stale air of the galley. She tilted the tin to its side and spotted a plastic pouch at the bottom. She reached in and pulled out the packet and held it up toward the light streaming in from outside the galley. It was filled with a white powder and was vacuum-sealed. She put the packet in the front pocket of her dress, put the tin back where she had found it, and slipped the lid on. She turned and walked up the narrow steps and out of the galley. She stopped by the instrument panel and smiled when she saw an open pack of cigarettes and a butane lighter. She picked up both and placed them in the front pocket of her dress.

Back at the rear of the boat, she saw the familiar blue sanitation truck of the island and recognized the man hauling off the garbage. "Giuliano," she said to the man, "give me a hand. It's been a while since I've stepped on and off a boat."

Giuliano smiled when he saw Nonna Maria. "I never took you for a sailor," he said to her. "But, then, nothing you do would surprise me."

"It's too late for me to learn new hobbies," Nonna Maria said. "Besides, I can't even swim."

Giuliano walked over to the rear of the boat, held out two hands, and lifted Nonna Maria back onto dry land. He was in his late thirties, with a strong upper body and a handsome face. His arms were tanned up to the base of his short-sleeved work shirt. "What were you doing on Pasquale's boat?" he asked.

"Saying goodbye to an old friend," she said.

"He will be missed," Giuliano said. "It won't be the same without seeing him walk these streets, with that dog always by his side."

"The garbage you just cleared out," Nonna Maria said. "Was it from the boat?"

Giuliano nodded. "I couldn't get to it yesterday. The carabinieri had the area blocked off."

"How many bags were there?"

"No more than two," Giuliano said. "I imagine what was left there from the night of the accident."

"Do you remember which two?" Nonna Maria asked.

Giuliano nodded. "The small ones in the white plastic bags. Pasquale always knotted them with a sailor's knot. An old habit of his, I suppose."

"Can I have them?" Nonna Maria asked.

"Now, what would you need with someone else's garbage, Nonna Maria?" Giuliano asked, tilting his head toward her. "There's nothing in there but coffee grinds and old rags. What else would you expect to find?"

"I don't know," Nonna Maria said. "I've never looked through someone else's garbage before."

20.

NONNA MARIA SAT on the stone bench outside Saint Peter's Church. The inside of the church was packed with friends and family of Pasquale Favorini, mourning his death as they prayed and sang hymns during his funeral mass.

Captain Murino walked by and sat next to Nonna Maria. "You're not going in?" he asked.

"I haven't been to a funeral mass since my husband died," Nonna Maria said. "And I only went because my children forced me to go. I wouldn't go to mine, but I'll have no say in the matter."

"It's just a way of saying goodbye," Captain Murino said.

"There are many ways to say goodbye, Captain," Nonna Maria replied. "We each choose our own."

"Buonopana is in the church," the captain said. "Sitting in the front next to Pasquale's wife."

"The surprise would be if he didn't go to the service," Nonna Maria said. "Some on the island believe his story and some don't."

"And I can safely put you down as one who doesn't," the captain said. "But as of this moment there is nothing to prove

86

he is guilty of anything other than falling asleep after a long day and night on the boat. No sign of a struggle, no blood on his clothes or body. Pasquale's death may be what it looks to be—an accident. We can't just wish it away. Not without proof."

Nonna Maria stayed silent for a few moments and then turned to look at Captain Murino. "The first mate was eager for Pasquale to retire, so he could take over the boat," she said. "Even Buonopana would admit to that."

"That makes him ambitious and perhaps impatient," the captain said. "That's still a far cry from murder."

"They were as close as any father and son could be," Nonna Maria said. "But even fathers and sons have been known to argue."

"Buonopana told my men he asked Pasquale numerous times to ease back on his workload," the captain said. "And the old man always refused. But there was no bad blood caused by it. They would discuss it and it would be forgotten the next day."

"Some arguments are not as easy to forget," Nonna Maria said. "And some things not as easy to ignore."

"You know something, Nonna Maria," the captain said, "something I don't. And it would be nice if you didn't keep it to yourself."

Nonna Maria nodded. "A friend told me about an argument Pasquale and Buonopana had a few nights before he died. It was loud enough for more than one person to hear."

"What did they argue about?"

"Pasquale was heard to say to Buonopana, 'You got yourself into this trouble, you need to get yourself out,' " Nonna Maria said. "And he warned him to stop using his boat to pay off his debts."

"What sort of debts?" Captain Murino asked. "And who does he need to pay off?"

"Young Buonopana likes to gamble, and like most gamblers he loses more than he wins," Nonna Maria said. "And that's when trouble begins. I don't need to tell you about the ones who come to collect such debts."

Captain Murino stayed silent for a few moments, looking up at the old white stone church. "And if Buonopana can't pay them off with money, they come up with another way for him to clear away what he owes," he said.

"I went on Pasquale's boat yesterday," Nonna Maria said. "I was brought there by a friend."

"Why would you do that?"

"It was my way to pay my respects," Nonna Maria said. "Some do it by saying prayers next to a coffin in a crowded church. I like to do it in my own fashion."

"That's only part of it," Captain Murino said. "You also went on board to look for something."

Nonna Maria nodded. "I didn't know what I was looking to find," she said. "But I had a feeling Pasquale's boat was being used for something that would bring trouble if it was found out. During the World War II years, that something was black-market wine. Moved from Ischia to Naples in return for much-needed money or food. Years later it was cigarettes and whiskey. Today it's something else. Something much more dangerous."

"And what would that be?" Captain Murino asked.

"Drugs," Nonna Maria said.

"And what makes you so certain that is what was being moved on Pasquale's boat?" Captain Murino asked.

Nonna Maria reached a hand into the side pocket of her dress and pulled out the sealed white packet she had found. She handed the packet to Captain Murino.

"It was hidden inside a coffee tin," Nonna Maria said. "It didn't seem to me like something that belonged there. Now, I don't know the drug world as well as you do. But it might well be the world young Buonopana found himself in. And it possibly could have led to Pasquale's death."

"My men searched that boat from top to bottom," Captain Murino said. "How could they have missed something like this?"

"They didn't know where to look," Nonna Maria said. "And they didn't know Pasquale and his habits."

"You should have come and asked me to send someone with you," Captain Murino said. "Simply to avoid the appearance of possibly tampering with any evidence you might have found."

"I didn't know there would be anything to find," Nonna Maria said. "And I didn't tamper with what I found. I'm handing it over to you."

"I'll bring Buonopana in for another round of questioning," Captain Murino said. "See if this time he paints us a complete picture."

Nonna Maria reached back into the front pocket of her dress and pulled out several empty plastic packets. "And when you do, show him these," she said, handing them to Captain Murino. "The bottoms of the packets are coated in a white powder. I pulled them out of two garbage bags that were in the back of a sanitation truck."

Captain Murino took the packets from Nonna Maria and glanced down at them. "How did you manage to get the garbage bags off a sanitation truck?"

"A friend did me a favor," Nonna Maria said.

"There were drugs on the boat and some possible residue in the garbage," Captain Murino said. "That's assuming the tests we run on what's in these packets come up as drugs and not something more benign. But if Buonopana was using Pasquale's boat to move drugs, then he would no longer be a person of interest. He would be the primary suspect in the investigation."

"What if he allowed others to use the boat to move the drugs?" Nonna Maria asked. "In order to pay off his debt."

"That's a possibility," Captain Murino said. "And the kind of men who move drugs for cash usually don't let anything or anyone get in their way. But if that were to be the case, it would not clear Buonopana."

"Even if Pasquale was killed that night by someone other than Buonopana?" Nonna Maria asked.

"If he's the one who let them on the boat," Captain Murino said, "then he's at the least an accessory to a murder."

"Pasquale loved his wine," Nonna Maria said, "as by now everyone knows. But there is one thing he never drank. Not as a young man and not as an old one."

"What was that?" Captain Murino asked.

"Coffee," Nonna Maria said. "Hated the bitter taste. A drop never crossed his lips. Which means that tin of coffee belonged to Buonopana. As does the packet that was in it."

"So, you do think the first mate killed Pasquale?" Captain Murino asked. "Either over drugs or some debts he was desperate to pay off?"

Nonna Maria shook her head. "I don't think he killed Pasquale," she said. "Despite their harsh words, he loved the old man, and nothing, not even the weight of heavy debts, would take him to such a dark place. And I don't think he was the one using the boat to move drugs."

"Then how else do you explain finding drugs on the boat?" he asked.

"There are many ways to pay off a debt, Captain," Nonna Maria said. "I would look to the ones Buonopana owed money for that answer."

"Did you find anything else on that boat, Nonna Maria?" Captain Murino asked.

Nonna Maria reached back into the front pocket of her dress and pulled out a pack of cigarettes and an expensive butane lighter. "These were in the back of the console by the instrument panel," she said, handing them to Captain Murino.

"A pack of Lords and a lighter," he said. "Both Pasquale and Buonopana smoked. They could belong to either one of them."

Nonna Maria shook her head. "Pasquale used his own tobacco and smoked a pipe," she said. "And Lord cigarettes are from England. Young men from Ischia don't smoke them, because they can't afford them. If they smoke, they smoke MS cigarettes, the cheapest brand you can buy. And if that lighter belonged to Buonopana, he would have sold it to help pay off his debts. Plus, it's not a young man's lighter. There are only two kinds of people who own a lighter like that. At least here on Ischia."

"Which two?" Captain Murino asked.

"Tourists and criminals," Nonna Maria said.

21.

NONNA MARIA'S HOME was filled with family and friends. Her children—ranging from the youngest, Franco, thirty-six, to the oldest, Francesca, fifty—were all working on their assigned tasks. Her two other sons—Joseph and Gabriel—were setting up the tables, carting one up from the first floor and sliding it in next to the one already in the living room. Her nephew, Carlo, followed in their wake, moving from first floor to second, bringing up two chairs with each trip. Her daughters Felice and Nunzia were doling out silverware, plates, platters, cloth napkins, wine and water glasses and setting a place and writing out names on small white cards.

Outside, the courtyard was filled with the laughter and screams of Nonna Maria's fifteen youngest grandchildren and great-grandchildren, all playing and running under the watchful eye of their older cousin Stefano.

In the kitchen, Nonna Maria reigned alone. She was preparing the largest meal she had in years: Grilled calamari, marinated eggplant, roasted peppers, sliced fresh mozzarella with strips of basil, and small peppers stuffed with fresh tuna made up the appetizers. The pasta was homemade linguine in a red sauce with clams and mussels, and the main course was chicken cacciatore and grilled Branzino marinated in balsamic vinegar, homemade olive oil, and thick cloves of garlic. There were a variety of roasted vegetables to be served as side dishes and two large salads—one chopped green lettuce dressed with lemon and olive oil, and the other made of garden tomatoes, red onions, hot cherry peppers, and basil, covered with red-wine vinegar and olive oil. Large loaves of bread still warm from the downstairs oven were stacked three-deep on a shelf behind her.

The dessert was a large cake baked earlier in the day by Rafael Minicucci, who owned the pastry shop a short walk from her home.

And there was enough bottled water and cold wine to satisfy a platoon. Nonna Maria had spent a good hour of her morning cutting up fresh peaches, skinning them, and placing them in decanters filled with cold white wine.

The feast was a surprise organized in honor of yet another grandson, Lorenzo, back in Ischia for the summer, on leave from his Navy service.

No one took more joy out of these events than Nonna Maria, and she always insisted they be a surprise, even as the grandchildren got older and came to expect a large dinner with family and then an assortment of gifts. It didn't matter to her. She and her husband had done the same for their children, and she believed the tradition would continue long after she was gone.

It also fed into Nonna Maria's talent for helping, nurturing, and caring for those she knew and loved, from family to friends. That unique ability, more than anything else, went to the core of who Nonna Maria was and why she was the one sought out to either celebrate happy occasions or offer aid during times of trouble.

"Do you think he'll be surprised?" her daughter Louisa asked. She, along with her husband and two children, lived in Pisa most of the year, coming to Ischia for the summer months, as did all of Nonna Maria's children who lived off the island.

"He's not expecting it," Nonna Maria said. "He thinks now that he's a grown man, and in the Navy, he's well past the age for these parties. But, out of all my grandchildren, he was the one who got the most pleasure from them. From the youngest age, it wasn't the gifts that mattered so much. It was seeing us all together, happy and there for him."

"Maybe because he lost his father at such a young age," Louisa said. "And Felice being a widow for so many years, it had more meaning for him than it did for the other children."

Nonna Maria turned away from the stove, all four burners heating pots and pans, her face red from the stifling warmth of the kitchen, and looked over at her daughter. "The reasons why are his to keep," she said. "All that matters is he remembers these days and will one day look back on them with a smile."

Louisa nodded and went out to gather the small children and rustle them to the downstairs bathrooms to wash up; then there'd be a fast run up the flight of stairs to the second floor and a secure hiding place.

Nonna Maria glanced out the kitchen window and saw her grandchildren and great-grandchildren rushing toward the bathrooms. She listened to the sounds of her own children in the next room, laughing and teasing one another, her family together in one place, safe and free from harm.

Nonna Maria looked from the entrance of the kitchen to the living room and for a few moments stared at the framed photo of her late husband, Gabriel. The photo was taken a few years after they were married, shortly before the birth of their second child. It was hanging as it always did, in the center of the wall across from the kitchen, a place where she could see it whenever she turned her head. When Nonna Maria sat to have coffee or wine or greet guests or just rest for a while, she always sat in the chair directly opposite her husband's photo.

Nonna Maria nodded and smiled at her husband. No one enjoyed these days, these meals, as much as he had. He would sit and tell his children and then his grandchildren stories about saints, feasts, and the long-honored traditions of the island they called home.

When Lorenzo was about six, maybe seven, he asked his grandfather, "Nonno, why is Saint Lorenzo called the patron saint of comedians?"

Gabriel lifted the boy in his arms and rested him on his lap. He set down his pipe on an ashtray and told him, "Saint Lorenzo was burned to death. They laid him down on a pile of thick wood and lit the wood with torches. Saint Lorenzo was lying faceup, the flames burning his back, neck, and legs. After about twenty minutes or so, he turned to those tending the fire and said to them, 'You should turn me over. I think that side's done.' "

Nonna Maria smiled at the memory while wiping away tears from her eyes. She then turned back to finish her work in front of a hot stove.

22.

NONNA MARIA STOOD next to Pepe the Painter, waiting as a beautiful young woman in a strapless summer dress bargained with him over one of his paintings. She had rich, thick, long blond hair, and her arms and back were red from too much time under the hot Ischia sun and too little lotion to ward off the burn. She spoke with a Northern Italian accent and was trying to use her looks and her smile to lower Pepe the Painter's asking price.

"I'm sorry, my bella signorina," Pepe the Painter said, "but the price is the price. Fifty euros. Any less and I might as well give it to you for free."

"But all I have are thirty euros," the young woman said. "And I love the painting so much. I will cherish it forever."

"Because you love it so much, I will let you have it for forty-five euros," Pepe the Painter said. "But not one euro less."

The young woman swung a shoulder bag off her arm and began to riffle through its contents. "I found another five euros," she said, announcing the discovery with great excitement. "So, I can pay thirty-five euros. Can we settle on that as our price?"

"I'm afraid not, bella signorina," Pepe the Painter said. "I can't let the painting go for less than forty-five. And even at that price, I'm giving it away."

"You know you're going to let her have the painting," Nonna Maria said to Pepe the Painter. "Just as you know that this young lady will magically find another five euros in her bag and you will settle at forty. But can we do it now and get it over with?"

The young woman stared at Nonna Maria and shrugged. She reached into her bag and came out with a second crumpled five-euro bill. "What made you so sure I had another five euros?" she asked Nonna Maria.

"Because I'm old and I've seen this back and forth many times before," Nonna Maria said. "It's an art form here in Ischia, and I do it myself every day with the merchants where I shop. I've even done it with Pepe. But we do it to save money. We never pretend we don't have the money when we do. Which I know you do. Even more than what he asked you for."

"How can you say something like that?" the young woman asked. "You don't know me, so how can you know how much money I have or don't have?"

"But I do know you," Nonna Maria said. "That dress you're wearing alone cost you twice what you're going to pay Pepe for his painting. Not to mention the shoes you have on. I saw them in the window of Michel's shop on Via Roma selling for eighty-five euros, and that's with his discount. And that bag over your shoulder is by a designer who has a home on this island, an apartment in Naples, and two other homes in the North. He didn't get all that property by selling his bags for little money.

And I'll do my best to ignore the two rings you have on your fingers, each one worth enough to pay for all the paintings Pepe has out for sale."

The young woman continued to stare at Nonna Maria, then looked at Pepe the Painter and handed him forty euros. Pepe smiled and nodded his thanks. "Would you like me to wrap it for you?"

The young woman shook her head, her eyes back on Nonna Maria. "No," she said. "I'm staying at the Excelsior. It's just around the corner. I can manage."

"Say hello to Giuseppe for me when you see him," Nonna Maria said to her as the young woman tossed the bag onto her shoulder and grabbed the painting with her left hand. "Let him know how happy I am to see he can still find guests who can afford to pay the four hundred fifty euros a night he charges for one of his single rooms."

Pepe waited until the young woman was out of earshot and laughed. "I knew she had the money," he said to her. "I was just having fun. Half my job is bargaining with the customers."

"Half your job is flirting with beautiful young women," Nonna Maria said. "You would earn a lot more for your work if you spent more time looking at their clothes instead of their bodies."

"Take that away from an old man and what has he left?" Pepe said. "I can tell you, not very much. Not very much at all."

"There will be another just like her passing your way before the night is done," Nonna Maria said. "This time of year, Ischia is filled with rich women, young and old."

"Well, then," Pepe said, smiling at Nonna Maria, "until the next rich beauty appears, it's down to you and me. I'm going to take a break from my work and pour myself a glass of wine from that bottle I'm sure you have inside your tote bag. We can sit by the wall next to the Villa Angela entrance. And there you can tell me what it is you wish to talk about. Though I can already imagine."

"I need you to tell me what else you've learned about Giovanni Buonopana," said Nonna Maria. "I've already let the carabinieri captain know about the argument he had with Pasquale a few nights before he died. And I know about the drugs, too."

"Those are excellent first steps," Pepe the Painter said. "But there's quite a bit more for you to know about the young first mate."

Nonna Maria reached into her tote bag and handed Pepe the Painter a bottle of red wine along with an empty tin cup. "I brought some food to go with the wine," she said to him as they moved toward the Villa Angela. "But before you eat, let's talk about Buonopana."

23.

NONNA MARIA'S ABILITIES to help friends in need had little to do with any special skills she had at breaking down clues or finding evidence in places no one had bothered to look. Nor was it her intuitive instincts that allowed her to put together the pieces of a given puzzle. While she did have a natural inclination to both those talents, they weren't the primary drivers of her success. What made her such a force to contend with was, above all else, how well Nonna Maria knew the island and its people. She could see beyond the obvious and look deeper and understand both the pain and the happiness layered under a local's skin.

She grasped the silence and sadness of the working poor of the island, watching as each summer they were surrounded by tourists without the weight of financial burdens, spending lavishly on dinners, expensive hotels, days of spa treatments, and nights filled with laughter and drink. Quietly and without much complaint, they put in their twelve-hour shifts and walked home weary and exhausted from another day catering to the well-heeled. There they would eat a meal, often made from plants grown in their gardens or on their small terraces, and spend what was left of the night in the quiet company of their loved ones.

When Nonna Maria walked the streets of Ischia, she saw beyond the new money pouring in from other parts of Italy and the outside world. She saw and recalled an island that had known war, misery, despair, poverty, and fear. These were ingrained in the Southern Italian soul and were an invisible part of Ischia, those times remembered now by a dwindling few.

Nonna Maria could look at the faces of the locals, both young and old alike, and see them for more than what they were. She didn't just look at the butcher and see a middle-aged man plying a trade he had learned as a young man and mastered through decades. Instead, she saw the young boy who had dreams of being an architect, designing structures that would forever stand the test of time. But, sadly, for him, life had its own design in mind. A family death and debts, an unplanned pregnancy, had forced him to change course.

She saw the women of Ischia, many looking older than their years, weighed down by too many children, wayward husbands, and no escape from the cycle of their lives. And she witnessed the struggles of the young, hoping to achieve the success that had eluded those who came before them, willing to work their way up from the menial jobs they were initially offered to a career that would earn more than they dared to dream.

But she also saw hope in the faces of the young, eager to take advantage of an island that had become a lure for tourists far and wide, their arrival and their money potentially opening the door to a wide range of possibilities that could never have been imagined by previous generations. They could expand their horizons and forge a career in work that had, for many reasons, been previously unavailable to locals. As proof of that, Nonna Maria needed to look no further than the signs she passed on the streets she walked. There were now more lawyers, accountants, bankers, and doctors on the island than ever before. And she smiled at the fact there was still only one dentist.

And she always saw the bright side of the island.

In the morning, sounds of women, young, old, and middle-aged, singing the songs taught to them by the generations in whose steps they followed. They sang as they hung out washed clothes to dry, as they lowered wicker baskets by rope down to the fruit peddler and chose the freshest from his wooden crates. She heard their singsong voices as they bartered with fish peddlers, store merchants, bakers, and butchers for the best price for the items they wanted to purchase. The music could be heard on every street, from every open window. They sang songs filled with love, passion, desire, humor, and heartbreak.

They were the songs of their island. And they were her songs, as well.

Nonna Maria smiled whenever she heard the mellow and romantic ballad "Parla Mi D'Amore, Mariu." It was her favorite song and one that her husband sang or played for her whenever the mood would strike. She would think back to one special night when, for no reason in particular, Gabriel took her in his arms and sang her the song. As he did, they danced together in the courtyard below their house, gazing into each other's eyes, seeing for those brief moments their younger selves, both knowing they were holding the one person they most loved in this world. On the stairs and through open windows, their children were scattered, staring down at their parents dancing in the courtyard, each with a wide smile on their face, a family united in the glory of simple pleasure.

Nonna Maria loved the mornings in Ischia, the smell of the mist being blown away by the heat of a rising sun, the strong odor of flowers and plants being watered, the sidewalks scrubbed and washed clean, the fumes of fresh-baked pastries and bread coming from the bakeries that lined the narrow streets.

This was her island, her home. And these were her people. She knew all of their blood feuds and deep friendships. Their distrust of strangers. Understood their deeply held religious beliefs. She knew that many of them pined for the simpler days of the past rather than the more complicated days of the moment. They were slow to embrace change and adapt. In many ways, the locals were like an angry old man who always longed for the days of his youth and the glories of his past, even though he knew that the mind tailored those memories in a light that shone far brighter than the reality in which they had been lived.

Nonna Maria knew very little, if anything, about history. She was never seen reading a book or a newspaper. She didn't watch television and had never been to the theater or the opera. She had no interest in sports or movies. She had not traveled to the big cities of the world or visited any historic places. That was not her life.

Her life was here, on the island of Ischia. Her life was among the people who lived and worked on the island. She understood their strengths and their weaknesses, knew their bad habits as well as their good. She knew who could be trusted with a secret and who could be counted on to spread gossip. She knew who would honor their word and who would be quick to turn their back on a promise made. She could spot the honest from those that weren't with one quick glance. These were her people, and she was very much one of them.

No one understood the island of Ischia and the people who called it home better than she did.

And that, more than anything else, was Nonna Maria's greatest gift.

24.

LUCA STEERED HIS boat as close to shore as he could get. He pressed a small silver button in the center of his control panel and watched as the anchor, which was located in front of the boat, rapidly unfurled and lodged itself at the bottom of the bay.

"Why are we stopping?" Anna asked. They were floating in an alcove somewhere between Forio and Serrara Fontana, a small, pristine white-sand beach less than a half mile away.

Luca turned away from gazing at the beach and looked at Anna. "I don't know how long Nonna Maria wants me to keep you on my boat," he said. "And I think it might be safer if you had someone stay with you at night. Someone you can trust."

"You and Nonna Maria are the only ones who know I'm on your boat, Luca," Anna said. "And I trust you to keep me safe."

Luca smiled at Anna. "I know you do," he said. "But if there is any chance of danger, you will need someone better than me. We can't count on luck to keep you safe. As Nonna Maria taught us since we were young enough to walk, luck has a way of running out. And that's where skill comes in. Some particular skills I don't have just yet. But I happen to know of someone who has those skills and can deal with any possible danger that might come your way. Someone you can rest easy with and trust."

"Who?"

"The Pirate," Luca said, turning back to look at the shore, smiling when he saw a small motorboat come roaring out from behind the sharp curves of a rock formation to his left. Manning the motor was a short, muscular, elderly man with a white beard, no shirt, and a red bathing suit. He had a red bandanna wrapped around his head. "And here he is now."

Anna and Luca watched as the old man navigated his motorboat closer to them, cutting his engine from several feet away and then easing it next to the side with a thin oar. "I hope you still have cool wine left on board," he said, smiling up to Luca. "I feel like I'm in a desert instead of on the water, floating under this hot sun."

He tossed a thick rope around one of the poles of Luca's boat and tied a knot to keep his motorboat moored, then pulled himself up and stood next to Anna, a wide smile on his face. "This must be the young lady Nonna Maria is concerned about," he said.

Luca nodded. "And who better to protect our friend Anna than the Pirate himself," he said.

Anna stared at the man, whose skin was the color of caramel. Despite his age, which she took to be somewhere in the seventies, he looked fit and hearty. The Pirate shook Anna's hand and then opened the cooler and pulled out a chilled bottle of white wine.

"There are plastic glasses in that small bin behind you," Luca said.

The Pirate quickly popped the cork and then took a long, soothing drink straight from the bottle. "Glasses are for guests," he said. "Not for friends. And besides, what kind of a pirate would I be if I didn't drink straight from the bottle?"

"Why are you called the Pirate?" Anna asked. She was somehow calmed by his presence. His beard was still wet from the spray of the water; his thick white hair was long and pulled back in a small ponytail, the bandanna double-knotted and hidden in back by the loose strands.

"To tell you the whole story would take longer than I have left to live," the Pirate said, taking a second swallow of wine. "But I've been called that for as long as I can remember, and for a man my age, that is indeed a long time."

Luca leaned against the instrument panel, his arms folded, happy to see his old friend. "I love going into crowded bars with him," he said to Anna. "A lot of the tourists look up and think I'm walking in with Willie Nelson. Having the Pirate next to me is one of the fastest ways I know to meet a girl."

"And I don't want you to worry," he said to Anna. "I'm a heavy drinker but a light sleeper. No one will get near you so long as I'm on this boat. You sleep down below, where you will be most comfortable. We'll send Luca on his way. He's earned a good night of rest."

"And where will you be?" Anna asked.

"In front of the boat," the Pirate said. "Hidden from view by the cabin. When I do sleep, I prefer to do it under the full light of the stars. All I need is a small pillow and a warm blanket."

"You have no other clothes?" Anna asked. "Just your bathing suit?"

"And a short-sleeved shirt in my boat," he said. "It has to be a chilly night for me to put it on, I must confess. But I always sleep with the shirt by my side."

"Why?"

"It's where I keep my sword," the Pirate said. "In case someone does come on board, looking to do you harm, he will at first see what I want him to see. A wrinkled, white-haired man in a bathing suit, old enough and drunk enough to be of no threat to anyone, let alone someone younger and stronger."

"That would be his first mistake," Luca said, turning to press the small silver button that would pull up the anchor.

"And his last," the Pirate said.

"He's called the Pirate for many reasons," Luca said, watching as the anchor reeled in and locked into place. "But the one that should matter most to you and allow you to sleep as soundly as a baby in a crib is this: No one on this island is better with a blade in hand than the Pirate."

"I was taught by the best," the Pirate said. "My father was originally from Sardinia; then he moved to Ischia. And Sards are taught how to use a knife from the time they take their first steps. He ran black-market goods all over these waters, my father did, in the years when it was a most dangerous occupation. The bottom of this bay is filled with the skeletons of those who made attempts on his life."

The Pirate lifted the wine, finished the last of the cool white, and tossed the empty bottle into the melting ice of the cooler. He smiled at Anna and laid a wrinkled hand on her right shoulder. "I'm going up front to take in the last of the sun and rest my eyes while Luca takes us back to port. And then, once we are docked, we'll eat together, get to know each other better, and then you go relax for the night. Leave everything else to me."

Anna looked from Luca to the Pirate and back. "Do you really think Bartoli will try to hurt me?" she asked, her voice breaking from strain.

The Pirate looked at Anna, his warm blue eyes giving her a small degree of comfort. "You're not his wife yet," he said, "so it would be foolish for him to try to bring harm your way. But he's probably angry you're being kept away from him. And that might lead him to lash out and attempt something foolish. But if he does, it would be a mistake on his part."

Luca looked at both of them for a moment, then kicked the engine to life, shifted his boat into gear, and headed for the main port of the island.

25.

NONNA MARIA WIPED a thin line of sweat from her upper lip with a twisted tissue and then placed it back in a front pocket of her black dress. It was a typical summer afternoon in Ischia, a cool breeze as difficult to find as money on the street, the summer sun at its hottest. Despite the heat and the nagging pain in her right leg, she continued to walk at her usual brisk pace. The streets were empty and the shops were closed, it now being the time when both locals and tourists enjoyed a few hours to sleep or relax or go for solitary walks on the beaches and side streets. If there was a need to get something done on Ischia, the hours between one-thirty and four-thirty were not the time to do it. The crowded island was as deserted as an old western town during that time.

Nonna Maria was not one to nap, and she never could come to terms with the custom of shutting stores and bringing an end to all activity in the middle of the day. It was an island custom and one that was practiced throughout Italy, but she found no comfort or pleasure in the loss of three valuable hours. So, while others slept away the afternoon, Nonna Maria went about her business without prying eyes watching her every move.

She stopped at a stone house situated between a branch of the Banco di Napoli and a shuttered laundromat. She stepped up to the thick brown door, grabbed the bronze knocker, and hit it against the shiny wood three times, then waited. She heard some rustling on the other side and then watched as the door slid open a crack. "It's me, Susanna," Nonna Maria said.

The door opened wider and an elegantly dressed, beautiful middle-aged woman stood in the foyer, her right hand on the doorknob. "Are you sure you weren't seen or followed?" she asked Nonna Maria.

"No one I saw either by foot, car, or scooter," Nonna Maria said. "And no one expects an old woman to be out at this time of the day. The sun is supposed to be too strong for us."

The woman smiled and stepped aside to let Nonna Maria come in, closing the door behind her as she did. She led Nonna Maria into a large parlor with two brown leather couches and three comfortable sitting chairs. Flowers and framed photos filled the fireplace mantel and the built-in bookcases that lined the room. A large flat-screen television was mounted on one wall, and two large bay windows looked out onto a well-maintained garden.

"I don't know what to offer you," Susanna said, smiling. "I know you never drink water, and I know you won't go near a cup of coffee that's not made in your kitchen."

Nonna Maria glanced at the large bowl of fruit in the middle of a wood-barrel coffee table. "Is that fruit from your garden?" she asked.

"The oranges and the peaches are," Susanna said. "Picked them off the tree this morning."

"I'll take a peach, but I'll have it later," Nonna Maria said. "After I have my dinner. But I will sit for a few minutes. When I was your age, the summer heat never bothered me. But with each passing year, I find it wears on me."

"I know you don't listen to anyone," Susanna said. "I've known you long enough to know that to be true. But you should be resting at this hour. A couple of hours of sleep would do you some good, especially at your age."

"I'll sleep plenty when I'm dead," Nonna Maria said. "But for now there's much work to be done."

"He's in the kitchen," Susanna said. "I closed the door so he wouldn't get out. I've never had a pet, so I wasn't sure if he would try to escape or not. Especially since he's never been around me before."

"A kitchen is a good place for a dog," Nonna Maria said. "And you were right to be careful. The only ones he's been around for the past few years has been old Pasquale and his wife, Fernanda. All he knows is the house and the boat. Anything and anyone else might cause him to run off."

"He's very sweet," Susanna said. "I gave him a bowl of water and a few crackers. I didn't know what else to feed him."

"They both probably fed him whatever it was they ate," Nonna Maria said. "Pasquale and Pippo were more than owner and dog. They were like father and son. And Pippo is lost without him. He roams the port and the nearby bars looking for him. He runs through their house, searching through every room and then rushes out again in search of his friend."

"And from what I hear, Fernanda is too distraught to care for him," Susanna said. "She wasn't well to begin with and has taken to her bed, mourning the loss of her husband."

"They are alone now," Nonna Maria said. "Both Fernanda and Pippo. And they must each mourn in their own way."

"It's sad," Susanna said. "That he would lose Pasquale to such a foolish accident." She brushed long strands of brown hair from her eyes, her face tanned, her slim body fitting snugly in a flowered wraparound dress.

"How did you find the dog?" Nonna Maria asked.

"More like he found me," Susanna said. "I was tending to the garden this morning, picking fresh fruit and watering plants, and there he was, snuggled under one of the lemon trees. He seemed exhausted, probably from running all over the port in search of Pasquale."

"Did you tell anyone you had found him?" Nonna Maria asked.

Susanna shook her head. "You are the only one who knows," she said. "You were a good friend to Pasquale, and you will be a good friend to Pippo as well."

"Little Pippo will have all the love and attention he needs," Nonna Maria said. "Not to mention food and drink. But before then I need him to help me find someone."

"Who?"

"The man who killed his best friend," Nonna Maria said.

26.

THE EARLY MORNING was quiet and still. Anna was asleep in the cabin of Luca's boat, the small wooden glass-paneled door locked from the inside. The Pirate was curled in a tight ball, his body jammed against the wood base in the center of the boat, his head resting on his balled-up shirt, the brass handle of the blade within easy reach. He was shirtless and still in his bathing trunks. A thin dark blanket covered his body from the waist down. It was ten minutes after three, and the only sounds in the port were the small waves lapping against the sides of the boat and the distant music still emanating from the Bar Calise.

The Pirate was asleep, but the light movement from the back of the boat was all he needed to open his eyes and reach for the handle of the blade. He stayed still as stone, his eyes open, keenly aware there was now unwelcome company on board. He eased the blanket off his body and wrapped it around his left hand.

He heard footsteps and whispers; two men were moving about the rear of the boat, one reaching down and tugging at the door to the cabin, unable to pry it open.

"It's locked," the Pirate heard one of them say in too loud a voice. "We could just break the glass window and get in that way."

"Would make too much noise," the second man said. "We can't risk being seen or heard. Besides, a cabin door lock shouldn't be hard to crack open. We have time. At least two hours before sunrise, if not more."

"We came in the night and should leave when it's still dark," the first man said.

"And that's what we'll do," the second man, clearly the senior of the two, said. "You, me, and the girl sleeping below will all leave together. No one will ever know we were here."

"Except for me," the Pirate said, stepping in behind the two men, startling them. They turned around to face him.

"Where did you come from?" the first man asked.

"Sardinia, originally," the Pirate said. "But that's a long story for another night and not one I like to tell strangers."

The Pirate stood in front of the two men, wearing only his red swim trunks and holding the thin dark blanket wrapped around one hand. His other arm hung loose by his side, the crumpled shirt wrapped around his hand and wrist.

The first man leaned against the cabin wall and smiled. "Are we supposed to be scared off by an old man in a bathing suit?"

The Pirate shook his head. "No, that shouldn't scare you off," he said. He then dropped the crumpled shirt and lifted the sharp blade clutched in his right hand, the light of a full moon catching the glint of the steel. "An old man with a sharp blade that cuts through skin and bone, maybe that should."

"There's two of us," the second man said.

"I'm old," the Pirate said, "not blind. There was a time, a few years back, on the Amalfi Coast, running cigarette boats, when I took on three at the same time. That one worked out to my benefit, not theirs. Not sure I could handle three again. But two? No problem."

"We were hired to take the girl," the second man said. "And that's what we plan to do."

"And I was asked to keep her safe," the Pirate said. "And that's what I plan to do. So it seems like a decision needs to be made. Now, I imagine what you're thinking. You rush me, knock me off-balance, and I drop the blade."

"Not a bad suggestion, old man," the first man said.

"Except for two facts," the Pirate said. "The first is, you can't afford to let me live, because I can identify you to the carabinieri. Which means you leave here as murderers. The second is, even if you were to knock me off-balance, I never drop this blade. That means one if not both of you will lose a great deal of blood and possibly a limb."

"You seem sure of yourself, old man," the second man said.

"It's the luxury of age," the Pirate said.

"So, we stand here and stare at each other until morning?" the first man said.

"Once the girl wakes up and opens the cabin door, there's nothing that prevents us from grabbing her and taking her with us," the second man said.

"The girl's awake," the Pirate said. "Has been for at least ten minutes now. From the other side of the boat, I could see into the cabin and caught her eye. She won't be coming out of that cabin door. Not while you're still on board."

"So, what, then?" the first man asked. "We leave? Walk away from you and the girl?"

The Pirate shook his head. "No, we wait, all of us—the two of you, me, and the girl," he said.

"Wait for what?"

Three carabinieri cars, sirens blaring, headlights on high beam, shot around the edges of the port and skidded to a stop in front of Luca's boat. "For them," the Pirate said. "I texted them a few minutes ago. Just in case you were tougher and smarter than you first appeared."

Four carabinieri officers jumped on the boat and grabbed the two men. Captain Murino stood off to the side, glancing up at the Pirate and smiling. "I have never seen you in clothes," he said to him. "No matter the time of year. Aren't you ever cold?"

The Pirate returned the smile. "Cold hands," he said, "warm heart."

"We'll take these two off your hands," Captain Murino said.

"Then my job for the night is done," the Pirate said.

The second man, held in place by two young carabinieri, glared at the Pirate. "You made a fool of us, old man," he said. "You've probably never used that blade in your life. Wouldn't know how to swing it if you had to."

The Pirate looked at the second man and, without much effort, lifted the sharp end of the blade and brought it down against the front of the man's buttoned blue shirt. In a single swoop, he sliced off all the buttons, watching each one fall harmlessly to the wood floor. The second man's eyes opened wide, and he let out a loud groan. There was no blood, only an exposed chest and the flapping of a now-damaged shirt.

The Pirate lowered the blade and stepped closer to the second man. "That was a preview," he said to him. "If we have the misfortune of meeting again, I'll make sure you lose more than your buttons."

The Pirate walked away from the man, nodded his goodbye to Captain Murino, and swung off Luca's boat and down to his motorboat. He pulled the thick rope from the iron mooring, sat in the rear of the boat, and kicked over the engine.

In a matter of minutes, the Pirate steered his way clear of the docked boats of the port and made for the open waters of a silent and still Bay of Naples.

27.

CAPTAIN MURINO WALKED alongside Nonna Maria as they made their way down the path leading away from the hospice located in the borough of Casamicciola. The captain and Nonna Maria had driven up to visit a mutual friend, Bruno Almanti, who was waging a battle against a cancer that would soon take his life. He had been Ischia's best shoemaker, taking over the practice left him by his father, Amadeo. He worked out of a large storefront in Ischia Ponte and took pride in his craft, never missing a day's work, taking great care to stitch together the shoes worn by many of the locals of the island. Nonna Maria would visit his shop often, buying sandals for herself and shoes for her children and, later, her grandchildren. She trusted in his work and valued him as a friend.

Murino was there to pay his respects. Almanti was his fiancée's favorite uncle, and he had always enjoyed his company at various family gatherings.

"It's a shame to have to see him in such a bad way," Captain Murino said. "He was a bull of a man. To see him reduced to pale skin and brittle bones saddens me. Loretta is heartbroken. She adores him."

"It's an end that awaits us all," Nonna Maria said. "There's no escaping it. But my memories of Bruno will always be pleasant. And we are best judged, Captain, by those we leave behind. Bruno leaves behind a beautiful family, including your lovely fiancée."

They turned a corner and were making their way toward Captain Murino's car. "Are you in a rush to get back?" he asked Nonna Maria.

"That's something I should be asking you," Nonna Maria said. "You're the carabiniere, not me."

"Sometimes I wonder," Captain Murino said, smiling.

He pointed to a small park bench shaded by a large pine tree. "Let's sit for a bit and talk," he said. "Then I'll be happy to drive you wherever it is you wish to go."

"If you're in a hurry, we could talk in the car," Nonna Maria said. "You drive and talk, and I look out the window and listen."

Captain Murino placed a hand under Nonna Maria's arm and walked her toward the park bench. "This won't take long," he said. "Besides, there is so much to distract me in the car—the chatter coming over the scanner, not to mention the crazed way the locals drive their cars and scooters. An accident waiting to happen. Here, we can sit, look out at the water, and talk without interruptions."

They sat on the bench, Nonna Maria looking out at the ships running up and down across the shoreline and at the nearby beach, crowded foot to head with hundreds of tourists and locals mingled together. "There was a time when we could throw rocks onto that beach and not worry about hitting anyone," she said. "Now it's so crowded you can barely see the sand."

"Is that a good thing or bad, you think?"

"A little of both," Nonna Maria said. "It's good for the locals to be able to earn enough to live and support their families. All the same, it takes a little away from what makes this such a special place. For me, at least. But I'm old, and I expect that is how old people are supposed to feel when they see so much that's changed in their lifetime."

Captain Murino looked over at Nonna Maria and leaned in closer to her. "I'm worried about you," he said. "My men have looked all over for Bartoli and haven't been able to find him. But I have no doubt he is still here on Ischia."

"It's Anna he's after," Nonna Maria said, not bothering to look away from the shoreline. "But she's well protected, as you discovered for yourself."

"He's come after you once," Captain Murino said. "He might do so again. If he can get to you, it will lead to her. Which, in my mind, puts you in danger."

Nonna Maria turned and faced Captain Murino. "He tried that once already and failed," she said. "And he will likely try it a second time. In which case, we won't need to find him—he'll have found us."

"I want to put you under surveillance," Captain Murino said. "If Bartoli does come after you, I want my men to deal with him. I don't mean any offense, Nonna Maria, but they offer much better protection than an old man with a sharp blade or a muscular young priest."

"The Pirate has faced off against men more dangerous than Bartoli and he's outlived them all," Nonna Maria said. "And

I've known that muscular young priest since he was a boy. Back then, his hands were more often closed into fists than held together in prayer. I appreciate your concern, Captain, but I don't need your men following me around."

"I didn't think you would embrace the idea," Captain Murino said. "They won't be in uniform and will respect your privacy. But they will be there to act should Bartoli come after you or hire thugs to do the work for him."

Nonna Maria smiled. "All along I thought I was a thorn in your side," she said. "I never thought you cared so much about my safety."

Captain Murino returned the smile. "Just looking out for my favorite honorary carabiniere."

"How about this, then," Nonna Maria said. "I'll go and talk to an old friend, explain my situation to him. Ask for his help. If he agrees, I'll have him follow me and keep me as safe as a baby in a warm crib."

"And you believe this old friend can offer you better protection than two of my best trained men?" Captain Murino asked.

"I would stake my life on it," Nonna Maria said.

"Who is this old friend?" Captain Murino asked. "Is it someone I know?"

"You've heard of him," Nonna Maria said. "But he's never given you or your men reason to go looking for him. And I will be happy to tell you his name, but before I do, I need to talk to him and see if he will agree to be my bodyguard."

Captain Murino stayed silent for a few moments and then nodded. "Very well. At least this way you don't have to come up with clever ways for my men to lose sight of you. An old friend, someone you know and trust, might be enough to keep Bartoli at bay."

"Especially this old friend," Nonna Maria said. "I'll talk to him after I get home. I might even bring the dog to see him. He loves dogs."

"What dog?"

"Pippo," Nonna Maria said. "Pasquale's dog. The one that was always on the boat with him, night and day, and never left his side."

"Where did you find him?" Captain Murino said.

"I didn't," Nonna Maria said. "He was given to me by someone who found him resting under a tree by her house. He survived that night and, other than young Buonopana, is our only witness to what happened on that boat that led to the murder."

"It has not been ruled a homicide, Nonna Maria," Captain Murino said. "At this point in the investigation, it is still considered an accident. We both have our suspicions to the contrary, but that's all they are. We have nothing close to a shred of evidence or, for that matter, an eyewitness that will prove Buonopana, or anyone else, murdered Pasquale Favorini."

Nonna Maria stood and looked down at Captain Murino. "Pippo was on that boat, and he saw everything that night," she said. "If Pasquale was murdered, then Pippo might be the one to lead us to the killer."

Captain Murino stood and waited as she hooked an arm under his left elbow. They started walking toward his parked squad car, the heat of the sun-soaked day making the air feel thick and heavy. "I never once doubted your many skills, Nonna

Maria," he said, smiling at her. "But I don't think even you could get a dog to talk."

Nonna Maria shrugged her shoulders. "I don't need Pippo to talk, Captain," she said. "I need him to let me know who killed Pasquale. He's a smart dog. He'll figure a way to tell me."

28.

NONNA MARIA HANDED a cup of melon gelato to Gian Luca, her youngest grandson. He took the cup, smiled, pulled out the pink plastic spoon, and dug right in. He was twelve years old, dressed in his usual summer outfit of shorts, short-sleeved T-shirt, and sneakers that lit up whenever he took a step. He was thin and wiry, with thick golden-brown hair, matching eyes, and an easy smile. To Nonna Maria, he resembled his father, her son Joseph, who among all her children was the closest in appearance to her beloved husband, Gabriel.

Nonna Maria smiled back at him. "Let's walk while you eat," she said, grabbing a handful of napkins from a canister on the La Dolce Sosta counter. "I told your mother I would have you home in time for your piano lesson. And we don't want to do anything to put her in a foul mood."

Gian Luca nodded. "I don't know why she makes me take lessons," he said. "I told her I don't want to learn how to play the piano. I want to play the drums."

"A piano makes less noise," Nonna Maria said. "That might be one reason. And your mother plays the piano, so she might want to pass on the tradition. It keeps her happy. That's all that matters."

They walked in silence for several moments. The streets were quiet and nearly empty, tourists and locals both taking a break from the afternoon heat. "Nonna," Gian Luca said, "can I ask you something?"

Nonna Maria glanced down at him and nodded. "I hide nothing from you, Gian Luca," she said. "You may be my youngest grandson, but you're also one of the wisest. I always want to know what's on your mind."

"I hear Mama and Papa talking," Gian Luca said. "They talk about how much they worry about you. They're afraid you might get hurt. They say you get involved in things you shouldn't. Things you should leave to the police. Is that true?"

"Some of it is," Nonna Maria said. "And your mother and father are not alone thinking I get in the middle of things that should be none of my business. But I don't want you to be afraid I will be hurt. That's not something you need to worry about."

"Why do you do it?" Gian Luca asked. "Instead of letting the police take care of it?"

"Most of the time, the people I help are friends of mine," Nonna Maria said. "Many of them are people I've known for most of my life. People who would help me if I needed it. And they usually come to me before they go to the police."

"Why?"

"It's easier for the people who live here to trust someone they know and who knows them," Nonna Maria said. "I suppose that's true about most people no matter where they live. But it is especially true here on the island."

"I don't want you to get hurt," Gian Luca said, finishing the last of his gelato. "I could help you, if you let me. Mama says you have some of your friends help you on these cases. So why can't I be one of the ones who help?"

Nonna Maria smiled. "I might have a job for you," she said. "But I need you to keep it a secret from everyone, including your mother and father. Can you do that? Can I trust you to keep a secret?"

Gian Luca ran a few steps ahead and stood in front of Nonna Maria. "You can trust me, Nonna," he said. "I won't tell anyone. I promise."

Nonna Maria reached out and embraced her grandson. "I have the perfect job in mind," she said. "An important job that will be of great help to me. I'll call your mother later tonight and ask if you can come and stay at my house for a few days."

Gian Luca released Nonna Maria and shook his head. "I don't think she'll say yes," he said. "I'm supposed to have piano lessons every day this week."

"Don't worry about the lessons," Nonna Maria said. "You won't miss any. And if I can't take you to them, I'll make sure one of your cousins will walk you there."

"I can get to my house by myself, Nonna," he said. "I'm not a baby anymore."

"I know you're not, Gian Luca," Nonna Maria said. "And I know you can get to your house by yourself. But there might be people watching my house, and we need to be careful. If you're going to help, you need to do as I tell you."

"Who is it that we're looking for?" Gian Luca asked.

"Who it is, I'm not sure yet," Nonna Maria said. "But what I do know is soon enough they will show their hand. And we need to be ready for when that moment happens."

"I'll be ready, Nonna," Gian Luca said. "You can count on me."

"I know," Nonna Maria said. "And I feel so much better now that I have you helping me."

"Is there anything you need me to do today?" Gian Luca asked.

Nonna Maria smiled. "Yes," she said. "Go home and take your piano lesson and play as well as you can. Put a smile on your mother's face. Making her happy is your only job for tonight. Will you do that for me?"

"Yes, Nonna," Gian Luca said. "You can come up and listen if you want."

"It will be better if you play for your mother without me there," Nonna Maria said. "I don't want her to think you're playing well just to impress me. And I also don't want to keep an old friend waiting."

"Who?"

"You don't know him," Nonna Maria said. "But if dangerous men are out to bring harm our way, we will need a dangerous man on our side."

"And your old friend is a dangerous man?"

"He is the most dangerous man in Ischia," Nonna Maria said.

29.

GIOVANNI BUONOPANA SAT on the cold wet sand of the tiny beach in Ischia Ponte, the glow of the lights of the Castello Aragonese at his back. It was deep into the middle of the night, the locals asleep behind shuttered windows and locked doors. The waves rippled in and out and cooled his bare feet. He was wearing a pair of knockoff blue jeans, a white polo shirt, and had a blue sweater draped across his shoulders, the arms twisted in a knot around his neck. Even though the night had cooled from the blistering heat of the day, Buonopana's arms and neck were coated in a cold sweat.

Two men stood above him, both smoking unfiltered cigarettes, one smiling, the other glaring down at him. "You need to get back to work," the one with the smile said. "The pipeline's beginning to go dry, and you are only halfway to paying us what you owe."

Buonopana looked at both men and shook his head. "The carabinieri are still investigating Pasquale's death and because of that have yet to release the boat," he said. His voice was shaky, a tremble to each word. "I can't be of any help to you without the boat."

"You have friends in the port," the second man said. "Go see if one of them will let you use their boat until the other matter is cleared up. The sooner you get back to work, the sooner you can put all this behind you."

The two men worked the black market, moving drugs, contraband cigarettes, and stolen cases of mineral water and wine from Naples to Ischia. They plied their trade under the cover of night, moving their shipments from one boat to another, the goods wrapped in waterproof containers and tied to the sides of a boat, unseen by prying eyes.

It was a practice that had been in play since the early years of World War II, and the profits helped sustain the underground economy of Naples and keep it both profitable and shielded from the eyes of the law. As with many illegal occupations in Southern Italy, especially in the more impoverished areas of the towns and cities, participation in the dark economy was often handed down from generation to generation.

"At last count, you owe close to six hundred euros," Luigi Beppo, still holding on to his smile, said. "And the longer you go without helping us move our goods, the higher your interest rate goes. You go another week or two without work, that number will be closer to eight hundred."

"You're acting as if all this is my fault," Buonopana said. "If you had let me deal with Pasquale, none of us would be in this situation. I would have explained the position I found myself in to him. He would have been angry with me, but he would have understood and helped me out. Instead . . . well, instead . . . he's dead. All because of you."

"And if you weren't an addicted gambler, you wouldn't owe

us money and we wouldn't be here talking to you," the second man, Angelo Narini, said. "So, if anyone's to blame for that old man's death, I'd say it was you."

Luigi Beppo walked closer to the water's edge and looked out at the dark and silent bay. He was the older of the two men, in his early forties, tattoos running up and down the front and back of his muscular arms. He was wearing a thin cotton short-sleeved shirt, beige cargo shorts, and brown sandals. He had worked the dark economy since he was a teenager. He had no formal schooling and had never held a job that didn't pay him in under-the-table cash. He turned to face the much younger Buonopana. "You think the carabinieri believe your story?" he asked. "That you were asleep and the old man slipped and fell overboard?"

Buonopana nodded. "As of now they don't have much choice," he said. "They think I was the only other person on the boat. And they knew Pasquale liked his wine and the older he got the more he drank. An accident was bound to happen sooner or later. Especially late at night out on the open sea."

"Yet they still haven't given back the boat," Angelo Narini said. He was in his late twenties, tall, thin, and with a long scar running down the left side of his neck, the result of a knife fight in a Naples prison several years back. He was the son of a Camorrista boss, the local branch of the Neapolitan mob. He had been arrested several times over the years, serving one three-year sentence for assault and battery and barely beating a murder rap, aided by the death of the one eyewitness. "Which, to me, means they haven't completely eliminated you as a suspect."

"That's not because of the carabinieri," Buonopana said.

"Because of who, then?" Beppo asked.

"There's someone else looking into the case," Buonopana said. "Someone who has both the ear and the trust of the carabinieri captain."

"Don't make us guess," Narini said.

"She's an elderly woman," Buonopana said. "Seems to get involved in everything that happens on the island. She was also a friend of Pasquale. She's been asking questions and even managed to get on board and search the boat."

"And what did this old woman find that the carabinieri couldn't?" Beppo asked.

"On the boat, nothing I'm aware of," Buonopana said. "But she now has Pippo."

"Who the hell is Pippo?" Narini asked.

"Pasquale's dog," Buonopana said. "He was on the boat that night."

"So we should be worried about a dog?" Beppo asked. "Unless this old woman can get the dog to talk, I don't see the problem."

"I don't know what she's planning to do," Buonopana said. "But she's not to be taken lightly. If there's a way to figure out what happened on that boat, then she will be the one to do it."

"Do you know this woman?" Narini asked.

"You would be hard-pressed to find anyone on Ischia who *doesn't* know Nonna Maria," Buonopana said.

"I don't think one little old lady should worry us," Narini said. "Let her snoop around all she wants. All she has is a dog and nothing more. That's not going to get her far."

"And no one but you knew we were on that boat," Beppo said. "So as long as you stay quiet, we stay invisible."

"Has she come around to ask any questions?" Narini asked.

Buonopana shook his head. "She's keeping her distance," he said. "At least for now. She's letting the carabinieri take the lead. But I have no doubt she'll find her way to me."

"Stick to your story," Narini said. "You do that, you have nothing to worry about. Nothing other than the money you owe us."

"We get back to work end of the week," Beppo said. "I don't want to risk losing any of our regular clients to other smugglers. Competition is tight as is; we don't want to make it worse."

"But what about Nonna Maria?" Buonopana asked.

"You worry about bringing our goods into port and paying off your debt," Narini said. "We'll worry about this Nonna Maria."

Buonopana looked up at both men. "I won't let you hurt her," he said. "I didn't stop you from killing Pasquale. I should have and I didn't, and that will haunt me the rest of my life. But I won't let you do anything to Nonna Maria. I will die before I allow that to happen."

Beppo glanced at Narini and then walked up to Buonopana, clumps of wet sand clinging to the sides of his sandals. He bent down and looked hard into the young man's eyes. "We can make that happen," he said to Buonopana. "One more, one less. It's all the same to us."

30.

THE LARGE ROOM was dark, dingy, and filled with slow-moving clouds of cigarette smoke. There was a strong smell that mixed easily with the cigarette fumes, dirty clothes blending with the stale stink of mildew and food left out to rot in the blistering heat. A thin cat was spread out on the floor, sleeping away the afternoon in a dust-filled corner.

The room was on the first floor of the last house on the port. The two-story structure was in desperate need of repair, and the stone steps outside its entrance were moist and moldy, due to the lapping of the waves and the thick blasts of humidity that covered that area of the port like a heavy blanket, regardless of the season.

Nonna Maria walked in, her eyes adjusting to the darkness. The only light in the room was a low-flickering candle in the middle of a rickety wooden table up against a wall to her left. She slowly made her way toward a cot at the far end of the room and saw the large, muscular man sitting on a thin mattress, his arms resting on his bare legs, an unlit cigarette dangling from one corner of his mouth.

"You shouldn't be in here," he said to her.

"And you shouldn't be living like this," Nonna Maria said to him.

The man took a quick glance around the room and nodded. "You're probably right," he said. "But it suits me. At least for now."

"It doesn't look like you get out much," Nonna Maria said. "You haven't been seen in any of the nearby bars in weeks. Or so the gossips tell me."

The man smiled, barely visible in the dim light. "Maybe I go out when the gossips are asleep. The less they see of me, the better."

Nonna Maria nodded. "What do you do about food and water?" she asked. "There doesn't seem to be much of it around here. Even the cat looks like it hasn't had a meal in weeks."

"We get by," the man said. "At this point in my life, that's the best I can expect."

"It doesn't have to be this way," Nonna Maria said. "You deserve a better ending than what you have now."

The man stood up and walked toward Nonna Maria. He was well over six feet, with massive shoulders, thick veins running down his arms, and legs that rippled muscle with each step he took. "This is how men like me end up," he said. "In rooms like this or locked inside a prison cell. It's all the same. And it's all deserved."

"For most men, that's probably true," Nonna Maria said. "But not for you."

The man looked at her and then turned toward the small makeshift kitchen on the other side of the room. "I would offer you a glass of wine," he said, "but I'm afraid my bottles are empty at the moment."

"I'll have some sent over from the vineyards," Nonna Maria said. "A five-liter jug of D'Ambra white. That should keep you for a while."

The man looked at Nonna Maria and nodded his thanks.

"But I didn't come to see you hoping you would offer me a glass of wine," she said.

"I didn't think you did," the man said, "but what I haven't figured out is why you did come here to see me."

"To offer you a job," Nonna Maria said.

"There's a word I haven't heard in a long time," the man said. "Now, what kind of job would a woman like you have to offer a man like me?"

"You still have connections with the men you used to do business with in Naples?" Nonna Maria asked. "The ones who work the dark markets?"

The man leaned his massive back against a rusty sink and folded his arms across his chest. "A few," he said. "As long as they're alive and not in jail."

"I would like you to get in touch with those that are living and free," Nonna Maria said. "Find out from them who is working the dark market in Ischia."

"That's the job?"

"That's part of the job," Nonna Maria said.

"What's the rest of it?"

"You heard about what happened to the tour-boat captain, old man Pasquale?" Nonna Maria said.

"I don't have to go out to hear about someone dying," the man said. "Not on this island. The way I heard it, he had too much to drink and fell off his boat."

"You believe that?"

"Doesn't matter if I believe it or not," the man said. "Pasquale's dead and that's all that counts. The how and why doesn't concern me."

"Well, it does concern me," Nonna Maria said. "And to find out what really happened that night on the boat, I could use your help."

"You didn't answer my question," the man said. "What's the other part of the job you're offering?"

"If any members of the black market were involved in Pasquale's death, they might not like the idea of an old woman looking into their business affairs," she said.

"So you need your back covered," the man said. "And you'd like me to be the one covering it."

"In a way," Nonna Maria said. "Sometimes these men go after family, and I don't want that to happen. So it's my family I wish to see protected."

"And you chose me why?" the man asked. "There are many out there you could hire. Younger, stronger, in better shape. Why reach out to a relic like me?"

"In your day, they called you Il Presidente," Nonna Maria said. "You were the most feared man on this island. On your word alone, people were left unharmed."

"That was a long time ago," Il Presidente said. "I'm now a shadow of the man you're talking about."

"A shadow is all I need," Nonna Maria said. "You may have

faded a bit, but your reputation hasn't. People around here still get nervous at the mention of your name—even the younger ones who have never laid eyes on you."

"I'm a hated man, Nonna Maria. And was once a violent one. No one likes me and no one cares if I live or die."

"I care," Nonna Maria said. "Years ago, as you recall, you helped me out of a situation that could have brought me harm."

"And you kept me out of a prison cell," Il Presidente said. "I still don't know how you managed that feat, and I don't want to know."

"It will remain my secret," Nonna Maria said.

"What makes you think black-market men were involved in Pasquale's death?" Il Presidente asked. "I've heard no talk of that."

"No one has," Nonna Maria said. "As of now it's either an accident or he was done in by his first mate. A young man named Buonopana. The carabinieri are still investigating, and the first mate is someone they are giving a closer look. But I don't believe either one is true."

"Why not?"

"Buonopana is known around the port as a man who likes to gamble," Nonna Maria said. "And I don't know many gamblers who win more than they lose. Which leads me to think he accumulated some debts. And, as first mate, he doesn't earn the salary that can help pay off those debts. Not when you include the interest that's often charged."

"So, instead of paying them back, he works off the debt by letting them use the boat to run their contraband into the island," Il Presidente said.

Nonna Maria nodded. "Just as you used to do when you were a young man," she said. "It worked back then, and it still works today."

"But, even if that's true, there's no way old man Pasquale would let them use his boat to run contraband," Il Presidente said.

"These men work under the cover of night," Nonna Maria said, "or so I've been led to believe. By that time, Pasquale has had his fill of wine. He lets the young man pilot the boat to Forio for fuel and then take it back to the port here, while he sleeps in one corner. He might never have known."

"They run the contraband off the sides of the boat," Il Presidente said. "They wrap them in waterproof bags, knot-tied in thick ropes. The goods are usually kept ten feet or more underwater, away from the eyes of any passing Coast Guard boats."

"The men meet the boat in open waters?"

"Usually," Il Presidente said. "They come up in a motorboat, tie the ropes with the goods on either side of the delivery boat. They are then given the money from the previous night's drop and disappear into the night. In many ways, a perfect system."

"But what if old man Pasquale wakes up during one of these exchanges," Nonna Maria said. "Demands to know what's going on. Maybe even threatens to go to the police. What happens to the perfect system then?"

"Money rules over life, Nonna Maria," Il Presidente said. "In that world—in any world, for that matter—that is one fact that never changes."

"Will you help me?" Nonna Maria said.

Il Presidente stayed silent for several moments. "If what you think is true," he said, "and drug runners are responsible for Pasquale's death, they will not let themselves be taken easily. They will do anything not to be captured."

"They'll be facing the police on one end and Il Presidente on the other," Nonna Maria said. "That might give them something to consider."

"I hope that's true, Nonna Maria," Il Presidente said. "For your sake as well as mine."

31.

NONNA MARIA SAT with her back against the stone wall, the doors to Saint Peter's Church open wide across the pathway. Inside, the church was crowded with those attending the noon high mass; the sounds of their singing mixed with the organist's musical renditions of the songs reverberated out to the patio and the streets below. Although Nonna Maria never attended services, she still took delight in the songs she had heard since she was a child. She was a spiritual person but did not consider herself religious, suspicious of the power the Church wielded.

"I like the saints," she once told her daughter Francesca. "From what I've heard about them, they were good people who tried their best to help those in need. It's easy to believe in someone like that. Popes, on the other hand, I have no use for. Some I've liked—John the Twenty-third and the current one—but most of them are as political as any senator in Rome. So, if I feel the need to pray or look to the heavens for help, it's the saints I turn to, no one else."

"Which saints?" Francesca had asked. "There are so many."

"Saint Jude, patron saint of lost causes," Nonna Maria said. "Giovan Giuseppe, patron saint of Ischia. Lorenzo, patron saint of those who make you laugh—what do they call those people?"

"Comedians," Francesca said.

Nonna Maria nodded. "That's it," she said. "Who doesn't need a laugh now and then? And, finally, Catherine of Siena."

"Why her?"

"She was brave and fearless and stood her ground," Nonna Maria said. "It's easy to respect someone like that, doesn't matter if she's a saint or not."

Nonna Maria turned her head when she saw Captain Murino walk up the steps to the small plaza. He sat down next to her and glanced into the church. "Does it count as going to mass if you are actually *not* inside the church?" he asked.

"That depends on who is counting," Nonna Maria said. "Besides, I don't feel comfortable in crowded places, churches or otherwise."

Captain Murino listened to the music coming through the open doors of the church for a few moments. "Bartoli knows he's being followed and is acting accordingly," he said. "We'll find him soon enough, but I still will need something solid to bring him in on. We can't prove he sent the two men on the boat to grab Anna. For now, he's playing his role to perfection."

"The concerned boyfriend desperate to find the woman he loves," Nonna Maria said.

"Exactly," Captain Murino said. "It's a part he's most likely played many times before."

"If he should attempt to contact Anna's parents, they know what they need to do," Nonna Maria said. "Let him act out his part and not give any hints they know his true motives."

"Bartoli is someone who is used to getting what he wants and also getting away with it once he has it," Captain Murino said. "He's avoided any charges in four cities in the North, including the one where my sister died. There may be others where he floated under everyone's radar."

"What did they think he was guilty of in those other three cities?" Nonna Maria asked.

"He goes after the vulnerable," Captain Murino said. "Both young and old alike. In Turin, he charmed an old woman out of thousands of euros of jewelry. In Venice, he conned a family in an insurance scheme, walking away with all their savings. And in Rome, he . . ." Captain Murino hesitated.

Nonna Maria stared at the captain. "He killed someone," she said.

Captain Murino nodded. "He worked his wiles to get close to a young woman," he said. "Both her parents were dead and left her well off financially. She was being cared for by her widowed uncle. Bartoli saw it as the perfect opportunity for easy money. The uncle didn't trust him from the start. He confronted Bartoli alone late one night. The following morning, the old man's body was found in a side street off the Via Veneto. He had been beaten to death. The carabinieri had only one suspect in mind but lacked any proof. And by then Bartoli had fled Rome."

"He's not an easy man to catch," Nonna Maria said. "He has a sense that when the oven is hot, it is best not to be near it."

"Every carabinieri contact I spoke to believes him to be guilty of everything they suspected," Captain Murino said.

"But they were never able to put together enough evidence to place him in custody."

Nonna Maria glanced over at Captain Murino. "But you've never been after him, and I have a strong belief you will be the one to end the chase," she said.

Captain Murino smiled. "With some help from you, no doubt," he said.

"He claims to love Anna, that he wishes nothing but happiness for her," Nonna Maria said. "Any other prospective groom, faced with a reluctant bride, one who has even gone into hiding, would by now have walked away. Would have realized it was not meant to be."

"And yet he persists," Captain Murino said. "But why? Anna's family is well off but not wealthy. Nor are they politically well connected in a manner from which Bartoli might benefit. He could easily write this one off as a lost cause and move on to his next target. But he seems determined to marry that young girl."

"And you keep asking yourself the one question we don't seem to have an answer to," Nonna Maria said. "Why?"

"Exactly," Captain Murino said. "Why did he single out Anna? There are many wealthy families on the island with daughters of marrying age. He could have set his sights on one of them. But he didn't. He focused solely on Anna."

"Anna's family is not wealthy," Nonna Maria said. "You're right about that. But Anna is."

"In what way?"

"It's not common knowledge or talked about among the locals," Nonna Maria said, "but Anna's parents adopted her from the orphanage in Naples when she was less than a week old. They've raised her as their own daughter, as they should, and love her dearly."

"And how does that make her a rich woman?" Captain Murino asked.

"When she was still a little girl, a relative came to the island to find her," Nonna Maria said. "To make sure she was loved and cared for. Turns out he was her grandfather, himself dying of a disease, and a very rich man."

"He left her money," Captain Murino said.

Nonna Maria nodded. "Quite a large sum, from what I understand," she said. "To make up for her being abandoned. It seems Anna's birth mother had a brief affair with a man visiting from another country. Since she was married, her family did all it could to avoid a scandal. Placing the baby in an orphanage seemed the easiest and fastest way out of their situation."

"Does Anna know about the money?" Captain Murino asked. "And about the adoption?"

Nonna Maria nodded. "She has been told everything," she said. "The family has kept nothing from her. The money is in the Banco di Napoli under her name, to be given to her on her wedding day. And should something happen to Anna after she was married, I have no doubt that money would find its way into Bartoli's hands."

"If many of the locals don't know Anna was adopted and even less know she had a wealthy grandfather and would inherit a great deal of money on her wedding day, then how would someone like Bartoli know?" Captain Murino asked.

"I don't believe he works alone," Nonna Maria said. "Not now and not when he was married to your sister. He works with someone who seeks out women for him to target. Finds out whether they have insurance or an inheritance that would come to him should they marry and then die."

"If true, this other person would need to be someone with enough connections to find out all this information," Captain Murino said.

"There's always someone eager to share someone else's secrets," Nonna Maria said. "Especially if they know their pockets will be lined with money once they do."

"My sister had an insurance policy through the company she worked for," Captain Murino said. "As well as a small trust left to her by one of my aunts. It wouldn't have taken much digging for someone to find that out."

"But in Anna's case, first you would need to know she had money and then you would need someone in the bank to tell you exactly how much," Nonna Maria said. "Two secrets not easily shared."

"Do you think Bartoli's partner is still on the island?"

Nonna Maria shook her head. "The partner's job is to find the target," she said. "Then Bartoli does the rest."

"And then they split the money," Captain Murino said.

"It requires a great deal of trust between Bartoli and this other person," Nonna Maria said. "And if the plan calls for Bartoli to always look and act like the grieving widower, then someone else needs to arrange the accident."

"Do you think his partner is a man or a woman?" Captain Murino said.

"Men kill more easily than women," Nonna Maria said. "And with less guilt. But women are smarter and have a better sense of who is more likely to be taken in by a charming stranger. And Bartoli seems the kind of man who likes to be around women and would be smart enough to find one to work by his side."

"So we now look for an invisible woman," Captain Murino said. "On an island crammed with tourists."

"For the moment," Nonna Maria said. "Keep turning over rocks, Captain, and eventually you'll find who you're looking for. Or we make it easy for them both to come to us."

"How?"

"I'm an old woman and you're a carabinieri captain stationed on an island," Nonna Maria said. "Bartoli has to believe he is so much smarter than either one of us. He does not fear you or me. You saw it yourself that night by the church."

"And so we use that to our advantage," Captain Murino said.

"For now, let's give him what he wants," Nonna Maria asked. "Let's set a new date for the wedding. Have Anna's parents get word to Bartoli that she would still like to marry him. She was simply nervous about beginning a new life with a man she barely knew."

Captain Murino stood and stared down at Nonna Maria. "You can't possibly want Bartoli to marry Anna."

"Just because a wedding date is set, Captain, doesn't mean there will be a wedding," Nonna Maria said.

Captain Murino put his hands inside his pants pockets and smiled at Nonna Maria. "You want to us to stop chasing the fox and allow him into the henhouse," he said.

"My husband was a shepherd," Nonna Maria said. "One spring season, his flock was being stalked and attacked by a wolf. He would spend many nights up on the hill, flashlight and shotgun in hand, lanterns lit across the property, waiting for the wolf to strike. But he never did. The wolf was keeping his eyes on my husband as much as he was on the sheep. And he always made his deadly move when he didn't see him on the hill, the glare of the flashlight and the lanterns lighting the fields."

"Did your husband ever capture the wolf?" Captain Murino asked. "Or did he move on to other pastures?"

"One night, my husband went into the fields without his flashlight and without turning on the lanterns," Nonna Maria said. "Instead, he lay still and motionless in the grass among the grazing sheep, surrounded by them. There was a full moon that night. Hours passed. My husband lay flat on his stomach, shotgun by his side, the sheep giving him all the cover he needed."

"Did the wolf show up?"

"Deep into the night, my husband heard movement coming at him from the ridge above," Nonna Maria said. "Sheep make very little noise walking on grass, and a wolf even less. But when a wolf is closing in on a target, his breath grows louder, feeling the kill that is only moments away. My husband reached for the shotgun, raised his head, and spotted the wolf closing in on one of the sheep. He rose to one knee and aimed his shotgun. The wolf turned his head and caught a glance of my husband. They stared at each other for a few seconds, both aware their game was now at an end."

"And you think Bartoli will fall into the little trap you are planning for him as easily as that wolf did with your husband?" Captain Murino asked.

Nonna Maria stood and rested an arm under Captain Murino's elbow, and they began to walk toward the steps leading away from Saint Peter's. "It's hard to trap a wolf," she said. "His senses are always on alert, on guard for any attack. That night my husband got lucky. The wolf was hungry, more interested in killing a sheep than in eluding a trap. If we get lucky, Bartoli will be more interested in taking a bride than avoiding the trap he's walking into."

"And when will you give me the details of this trap you're planning?" Captain Murino asked.

"I need to go and talk to some friends before I can do that," Nonna Maria said. "And I need a favor from you before I do."

"Name it."

"I need any information you can get from the carabinieri in Florence about the car your sister was driving the night she died," Nonna Maria said.

"And you would prefer no one but me knows you have that information," Captain Murino said. "And that I don't ask which of your friends sees what's in that report."

Nonna Maria smiled. "Now you're not thinking like a carabiniere," she said. "Now you're thinking like one of us."

32.

NONNA MARIA WATCHED as her twelve-year-old grandson, Gian Luca, tossed a ball to Pippo. The small dog, always eager to please, ran full tilt in the courtyard outside her home, grabbed the ball in his mouth, and raced it back to Gian Luca. "He's very smart, Nonna," Gian Luca said in between tosses. "When he needs to go out, he moves to the door and waits for me. And when he's hungry, he walks to the empty bowl next to where I keep his fresh water. He sits and stares at me but never barks."

"Pasquale trained him well," Nonna Maria said. "And you're very good with him. I always trust a person a dog likes. But I never trust one a dog doesn't. They have a sense about people and can tell good from bad faster than we can."

"Can we keep him, Nonna?" Gian Luca asked. "I've always wanted a dog."

"That's a talk we can have later," Nonna Maria said. "For now, enjoy his company while he's with us. You're not only helping me by taking care of him, but Fernanda, too. She's not well, but was happy to hear that Pippo was in good and trusted hands."

Nonna Maria walked over to a large wooden rocking chair

and sat down on the thick, soft pillows that covered the seat as well as the back. The rocking chair had been her mother's and before that belonged to her grandmother. Across these many years, the chair had been repaired more times than she could recall, her husband even going so far as to rebuild the bottom portion and reinforce the back panel.

As she rocked back and forth, giving some relief to her bothersome leg and hip, she thought of Anna and the untenable situation with Bartoli. Anna was about the same age as Nonna Maria had been when she got engaged to Gabriel. The thought alone brought back many happy memories of her years spent in the company of the only man she'd ever loved.

Even back then there were men like Bartoli, eager to take advantage of young women on the island, but it was harder in those years for a stranger to come to Ischia and work his charms or his potions on an innocent and expect to get away with it. The island was a peaceful place in those years, home to fishermen, shepherds, shoemakers, fruit peddlers, winemakers, and their families. What Ischia lacked in wealth, it made up for in community, friends, and relatives living together miles removed from the turbulence, violence, and uncertainty of big-city life.

Nonna Maria and her husband would often go on long walks together, a habit that began during their teenage courtship and continued throughout the years of their marriage and the birth of their children. They would stroll along the Lido in the late evening, hand in hand, going over any issues that needed to be settled or laughing off the latest neighborhood gossip or, more often than not, simply finding comfort in each other's company. They were more than husband and wife in love. They were partners fully committed to each other, and they were best friends.

"We were two working together as one," Nonna Maria said to her older sister, Giovanna, a few years after her husband's death. "And it was that way from the beginning. I was one of the lucky ones. We both were. We had each found our person, the one we belonged with. People search for that one person their entire lives without success. I found mine here on Ischia, less than a mile from my home."

Nonna Maria had been a widow now for twenty-five years, and while she still mourned the death of her husband, she found solace and comfort in the company of her children, grandchildren, great-grandchildren, and her many friends spread throughout the island. And she took great pride and satisfaction in the fact that the people of Ischia would come to her in their time of need. It could be a task as simple as convincing a hard-hearted landlord to give a single mother a few extra weeks to make good on the rent or a matter that was much darker in nature, such as the two issues she found herself currently in the middle of resolving.

She turned away from her thoughts and watched Gian Luca walk toward her, holding the ball in his right hand; the dog was lying flat on the cool ground, his face on the curved wood of one of the chair's rockers. "I think Pippo's had enough of chasing after the ball," Gian Luca said. "I'm going to let him rest, then feed him dinner earlier than I usually do."

"Let him nap after he eats," Nonna Maria said. "You along with him. It will do you both some good."

"Okay if he sleeps on the bed with me?" Gian Luca asked.

Nonna Maria smiled. "I would be surprised if this was the first time he did that," she said.

Pippo lifted his head and moved closer to Nonna Maria, rubbing one side of his body against her legs. She reached down and petted the dog, watching as he rolled onto his back and reveled in her caress.

"He likes you as much as he likes me," Gian Luca said.

"But still, he must miss his best friend, Pasquale," Nonna Maria said. "They were together for the longest time. When Pasquale first got him, Pippo was such a tiny puppy, you could put him inside your coat pocket."

"I'm sorry about what happened to Pasquale," Gian Luca said. "I know he was your friend and I know how much he loved Pippo."

Nonna Maria stood and embraced her grandson. "He was a good friend to me and to Pippo," she said. "And I think very soon Pippo will prove to be more than just a loving friend to Pasquale. And much more than just a dog."

"What else would he be?" Gian Luca asked.

"Your truest friend," Nonna Maria said.

33.

FREDERICO THE MECHANIC leaned against the wall of his garage, a cigarette in one hand and the carabinieri report in the other. He was short, bald, in his late forties, and his arms and hands had the marks of his profession—dark stains on brown skin, fingers marked with oil and grease, elbows scraped raw from resting flat on a concrete floor. When he heard the door open, he looked up to see Nonna Maria carefully avoiding any oil puddles and decade-old tools.

"I can see why they thought it was an accident," he said, looking down at the report. "The car smashes against a side of a truck, flips over, lands in the ravine, catches fire, any evidence gone up in smoke."

"Tell me how it wouldn't be an accident?" Nonna Maria asked.

"Well, lucky for me, not every part of the car was burned beyond recognition," Frederico the Mechanic said. "And the carabinieri mechanics didn't look as closely as they should have. For one thing, there was a small hose lodged in the exhaust that should not have been there."

"What does that do?"

"If the hose was pressed through an opening in the trunk into the rear seats, it would give off carbon monoxide fumes," Frederico said. "On a rainy night, with the windows closed, that would have been enough to make the driver woozy and cause her to lose control of the car and smash into the truck."

"And once it crashed, flipped, and caught fire, the smell of the fumes would have floated out the broken windows," Nonna Maria said.

Frederico nodded. "And the lining of the brake pads had been tampered with," he said. "The minute she felt her car skidding and hit the brakes, the car wouldn't have stopped because it couldn't stop."

"Like driving over black ice," Nonna Maria said.

Frederico the Mechanic smiled. "I forgot you know a bit about cars," he said. "I remember you coming into this shop when my grandfather worked here. You would bring him his lunch and he would sit you on the bench next to him and answer all your questions."

"He was a good man and a patient one," Nonna Maria said. "Because I asked him a lot of questions about the cars in this shop and I learned a great deal from him."

"And yet you yourself never owned a car," Frederico said.

"In those years, not many women on the island did," Nonna Maria said. "And I have legs. They take me wherever I need to go."

Frederico the Mechanic walked over to Nonna Maria and handed her the report. "The crash and the fire are what killed this woman," he said. "The carbon monoxide and the faulty brake lining caused the car to swerve, hit the truck, and flip.

The car was less than two years old. Yet one of the tires, the right front one, had very little tread on it. That can only mean someone changed out one of the new tires with one that would have little traction, especially around curves and in bad weather. Add it all up and this tells me it wasn't an accident."

"Anything else in the report I need to know?" Nonna Maria asked.

"Two days before the crash, the car had been checked and passed inspection," Frederico the Mechanic said. "There's a copy of the invoice and the sticker in the report. I don't know who brought the car in. But I know who picked it up and signed it out."

"Her husband?" Nonna Maria said.

"If his name is Andrea Bartoli, then the answer is yes," Frederico the Mechanic said. "So, either the damage to that car was done by someone at the shop or it left there clean and was done by the man who drove it out."

34.

NONNA MARIA WALKED up the small gangplank and onto the lower deck of the *Lucia Bianca*. Buonopana was in the cabin of the boat, the wood doors open, an endless array of wires exposed. He was working on them with a large screwdriver. He pulled his head out and looked down the short flight of steps and saw Nonna Maria.

She looked at him and smiled. "I'm glad the carabinieri freed up the boat," she said.

Buonopana stood up, reached for a soiled rag, and wiped lines of grease off his hands and wrists. "She needs some work," he said. "But nothing I can't handle. Pasquale trained me well—like a son, really."

Nonna Maria rested a hand on one of the guardrails and nodded. "And where do you stand with the carabinieri?" she asked.

"I'm a suspect," he said. "At this point, the only suspect they have. I'm not sure they believe what I told them happened that night."

"If it's the truth," Nonna Maria said, "there's no need for you to worry."

"You believe me, don't you, Nonna Maria?" Buonopana

asked, his lean body tense, his voice on the verge of cracking. "You must believe I wouldn't do anything to hurt Pasquale. Let alone let him drown at sea."

Nonna Maria stared at the young man for several moments. "I believe *you* would not do anything to harm Pasquale. But there are people who might not feel as you do. And I believe you know those people."

Pasquale sat on the top step leading to the cabin. His arms dangled by his sides and his head was lowered, his shoulders shaking with uncontrollable sobs. "I never thought they would do what they did," he said between gulps of breath. "I never meant for any of it to happen. It was me they wanted. Not Pasquale. I tried to stop them, Nonna Maria. You must believe me. I tried, but it all happened so quickly."

"It doesn't take long for someone to die," Nonna Maria said. "Especially an old man with a stomach full of wine."

"I'm so afraid, Nonna Maria," Buonopana said. "If I tell the carabinieri the truth about that night, these men will end my life as they did Pasquale's. If I don't speak the truth, then I will be sent to prison. Either way, I'm ruined, and I have no one to blame but myself."

"You owe these men money?" Nonna Maria asked. "Money you lost gambling."

Buonopana nodded. "I told them I would pay every euro I owed," he said. "And that I was holding up my end of the deal until I had the money to give."

"And what deal was that?" Nonna Maria asked.

Buonopana lifted his head and wiped the tears from his eyes with a sleeve of his gray T-shirt. "They were using our boat as a transport," he said. "Once a week, they would meet us out at sea, on our way to Forio to gas up for the next day. By that hour of the night, Pasquale would be sound asleep. Not even the sound of a motorboat coming alongside us was enough to wake him."

"And Pasquale never saw the drugs?"

Buonopana shook his head. "They were tied down and hung from the side of the boat," he said. "Wrapped in waterproof bags. Once we docked back in the port, I shook Pasquale awake and we headed home. In the early morning, the port is empty, not a soul to be found. That's when the drugs were lifted out of the water and taken away."

"And you were to do this until you paid off your debt to them?"

"Along with the few euros I was able to give them each week," he said. "But with the interest rates they charge, it's almost impossible to keep up with the weekly payments. Letting them use the boat as a drug drop shaved a hundred euros a week from what I owed."

"How much did you owe them?" Nonna Maria asked. "And how much of the debt is left?"

"I'm ashamed to tell you," Buonopana said. "I'm such a fool to have gambled as much as I did. Look at the harm and trouble it caused."

"How much?"

"Initially, two thousand euros," he said. "It's now down to a little less than six hundred."

"Do the carabinieri know any of this?" Nonna Maria asked.

"They know about my gambling debts," he said. "And they

suspect the boat was being used to move drugs. But they still don't know there were other men on the boat the night Pasquale died. I was afraid to tell them, Nonna Maria. Eventually, I fear, they'll piece it together. I've let everyone down, everyone that cares for me."

"No," Nonna Maria said. "Not everyone. Just the one man who loved you and gave you a living. You may have had your disagreements, the two of you, that's only natural. Our friend was not the easiest man to get along with, and there must have been times when he drove you mad. But there is no doubt he treated you as a son. And he did not deserve the death he was given."

"It happened so fast," Buonopana said. "I would have stopped them if I could. I didn't hear Pasquale wake up, and by the time I did, one of the men had tossed him against the side of the boat. He hit his head and lay still for a moment. That's all the time they needed to toss him over the side."

"These men," Nonna Maria said, "you've seen them before? Are they always the ones who bring the drugs?"

"Yes," he said. "They're from Naples, the two of them."

"And how did they come to have your gambling debts?"

"The man I placed my bets with sold my debt to them," he said. "It's a common practice in Naples. The number man gets back what is due him and the men in Naples collect even more than they paid out, due to the high interest they charge on the money owed."

"Are you planning to take the boat out again?" Nonna Maria asked.

"I was hoping to," he said. "It's the height of season and, as it was, I had to hand off a week's worth of bookings to other tour boats. If I am going to keep running Pasquale's boat, I'll need to earn money to care for it. Not so much for me. But for his family."

"And the drug business?" Nonna Maria asked. "Are you going to keep that going, too?"

Buonopana shook his head. "I've disgraced myself already," he said. "I will never let those men near this boat again. I'll find another way to pay them back."

"If you do that, they will get away with murder," Nonna Maria said. "And you might well end up in a prison cell. We can't let Pasquale's death go without the punishment it deserves."

"You don't understand these men, Nonna Maria," he said, his fear practically visible. "They will stop at nothing. Their reach is beyond anyone's control. If they don't kill me for betraying them to the carabinieri, then they'll harm members of my family. I cannot let that happen. And you can't, either."

"I understand these men more than you know," Nonna Maria said. "Many years ago, men like the ones who killed Pasquale went after my husband. They demanded a monthly payment from him in return for guaranteeing the safety of his flock."

"Did he pay them?"

"Not one lira," Nonna Maria said. "The matter was settled and they never bothered my husband again."

"Settled how?" he asked.

"That's a story for another time," Nonna Maria said. "For

this story to end the way it must, you need to trust me and do what I ask. Can I count on you to do that for me? For Pasquale?"

Buonopana slowly nodded his head. "What is it you need me to do?"

"Get in touch with these people," Nonna Maria said. "Tell them you are ready to make another pickup. Arrange it for day after tomorrow."

"I'm afraid of these men, Nonna Maria," he said. "They are ruthless when it comes to their business. They live only to make money. I don't know if I can do what you ask on my own."

Nonna Maria rested a hand on the young man's right arm. "Don't worry," she said. "You will not be alone. You have my word."

35.

LUIGI BEPPO AND Angelo Narini sat in a back table at the Bar Calise, both hidden from view by the thick leaves and branches of overhead trees. They were nursing Johnnie Walker Blue on the rocks and listening as Aldo Poli played electric piano and sang songs in English and Italian. The tables were all filled and the dance floor was crowded, as a wide mix of tourists, elderly locals, and young couples blended together.

"This place never closes, they tell me," Beppo said. "They must take in a fortune. People come here for their breakfast, then grab something to eat in the afternoon, and then at night, drinks, gelato, and dancing. It's a gold mine."

"So what?" Narini said. "None of it goes into our pockets, so why should we care?"

"Maybe this is something we should get Naples in on," Beppo said. "The bosses are always looking for new ways to bring in money. And, even better, this place would be a clean way to do it."

"Forget about that," Narini said. "Our people in Naples already know about this place—it's been here forever. None of this concerns us. We got to get back to moving the supply from

Naples to the island, and I don't know why we're waiting. The carabinieri freed up the boat more than a day ago."

"What about the old woman?" Beppo asked. "What do we do about her?"

"If the carabinieri can't figure out how the captain of the boat died, what makes you think some old widow can?" Narini asked.

"She's still asking around, and that's something we need to be aware of," Beppo said. "She could be a problem, old widow or not."

"Let her ask all the questions she wants," Narini said. "The only one who knows what happened on that boat other than the two of us is the first mate, and he's too afraid to say anything to anybody."

"We better hope he stays afraid," Beppo said. "Plus, he might not talk to the carabinieri about what happened, but he might open up to the widow."

"Why would he do that?"

"She's a local, probably somebody he's known since he was a kid," Beppo said. "Which might make her somebody he trusts, and if that turns out to be the case, as bad as it would be for the first mate, it could end up being worse for us."

"He's got too many debts on his head to worry about," Narini said, polishing off the last of his drink and making several attempts to get a waiter's attention for a refill. "And the only chance he has to pay the money back is to get the drug runs started up again."

"I still would feel better if this widow would sit home and mind her own damn business," Beppo said.

"How much do you know about her?"

"Enough to know she could be a problem," Beppo said. "Folks around here go to her with their problems, and she helps them find a way out. Been doing it for a few years now. And she's old enough to know everybody somebody like her needs to know. You hear tell around here, she carries more weight than the carabinieri."

"So, what are you suggesting?" Narini asked. "I'm not looking to beat up an old woman, if that's where your head is."

Beppo shook his head several times. "No, no, I'm not suggesting that at all," he said. "We put one old man in the sea as it is. Who the hell needs a reputation like that?"

"What, then?"

"She's got family—pretty big one, from what I understand," Beppo said. "There's a weak link in any family. We find who that is, then maybe we get her to stop looking into what happened on the boat that night."

"We don't have time to waste chasing down an old woman's relatives," Narini said. "What we need to do is get Buonopana to put that boat back out to sea so we can move on to our business. Let the old lady look all she wants. As long as the kid holds to his story, we have nothing to be worried about. Not from her and not from the carabinieri."

"I guess I don't have as much trust in the first mate as you do," Beppo said. "And if anybody can get him to talk, that old lady would be the one."

"He was there that night, just like we were," Narini said. "That makes him as guilty as if he threw the captain over the side. That plus the fact he's carrying his weight in debts are reasons enough for him to keep his mouth closed. No matter how much the old lady tries to get him to talk."

"Maybe so," Beppo said. "But I would feel a lot better if we could somehow get her out of our way."

"You worry too much," Narini said. He pushed back his chair, stood, and pulled a twenty-euro bill from his pants pocket and dropped it on the table. "I'm tired of trying to get a waiter's attention. Let's go find a place where they like to serve drinks."

"And then, first thing tomorrow, we go back and see the first mate and tell him to get that boat on the water this week," Beppo said, easing out of his chair.

"And we deal with the old lady only *if* we need to deal with the old lady," Narini said. "For now, let her snoop around as much as she wants. There's nothing for her to find and nobody for her to point a finger at. She doesn't even know we exist."

Beppo and Narini walked out of the Bar Calise and eased into the thick crowd of teens, tourists, and locals either coming in or walking out of the main entrance. They made a right turn and headed toward the port, a leisurely ten-minute walk away.

Il Presidente, resting with his back against the stone walls of the Bar Calise, watched as they left and turned toward the port. He moved away from the wall and began to follow in their wake, a brown fedora on his head and an unlit cheroot jammed into a corner of his mouth. He was wearing dark jeans, a long-sleeved dark button-down shirt, and a pair of snakeskin cowboy boots he had won in an all-night poker game years ago in a Naples bar.

He kept a safe distance from the two men but never let them out of his line of sight. Il Presidente had been up against men such as these many times in his life and knew they would not let anything stand in the way of their profits. Nonna Maria had her way of dealing with such men, and he would, for now, do as she had requested.

But if these men or any others like them tried to bring harm to Nonna Maria, then Il Presidente would handle them the way he always had when confronted by their likes. He would follow the custom that men like him, who had spent years toiling in a cold and brutal profession, had long come to respect and understand.

Blood begets blood.

36.

THE FEAST OF Saint Anne was in full celebration. The waters of the port were teeming with boats decorated in a variety of colors and symbols; a shoulder-to-shoulder crowd packed the path to the castle and the narrow streets of Ischia Ponte; the castle itself was encircled with thick piles of wood and straw that had been set ablaze, filling the moonlit sky with billows of thick brown smoke. A thunderous fireworks spectacular was on display, and in all corners, musicians played songs ranging from contemporary rock to decades-old romantic ballads. It was one of the biggest feasts held on Ischia and had, over time, grown to become one of the highlights of the summer season.

Captain Murino watched the fireworks display from the rear of one of the largest carabinieri boats covering the harbor. Nonna Maria stood next to him, a thick black shawl spread across her shoulders, helping to ward off the chill coming at them from the choppy waters of the bay. She looked up at the various shapes and sizes the fireworks took on, lighting up the night sky, the applause of the onlookers below echoing off the waters.

"Has it changed much across the years?" Captain Murino asked.

Nonna Maria nodded. "The crowds are bigger and the fireworks are more impressive," she said. "And there are more boats in competition and the music is louder. But this night still feels special, and I don't think that will ever change."

"I've looked forward to this feast day every year since I was transferred to Ischia," the captain said. "It remains so much a part of what makes this island memorable. And you don't need to be a local to appreciate it."

Nonna Maria looked out across the waters of the bay at the vast array of people milling about, walking or stopping to listen to the music, looking at the fireworks or the spectacle of large billows of smoke coming off the tiers of the massive castle. "He's out there, somewhere in that crowd," she said to the captain without looking at him. "Deciding what his next move will be."

"We know his next move," the captain said. "He'll be in front of the altar of Saint Peter's, waiting for his reluctant bride-to-be to make her entrance."

"You think he believed Anna's parents?" Nonna Maria asked. "Were they able to convince him their daughter was just a young woman fighting off a case of nerves?"

"From what I've been told, they played their parts well," Captain Murino said. "Her mother calmly assuring Bartoli that she herself had hidden from her husband of three decades weeks before their marriage, not because she wasn't in love but because she, like all women Anna's age, found the idea of committing a life to one man frightening."

"And the father?"

"He had the easier of the two roles," the captain assured her.

"That of the wise father who knew his daughter would come to her senses and marry the man she loved."

Nonna Maria looked away from the activity around the bay and over at the captain. "And Bartoli believed them?" she asked.

"One of my men was there, dressed as a civilian, mingling with the other family members surrounding Bartoli," Captain Murino said. "He seemed apprehensive at first. But when the pastries and the wine and spumante were brought out to celebrate the occasion, he relaxed and by evening's end seemed to be enjoying the festivities."

"Did he not wonder why Anna herself wasn't there?" Nonna Maria asked.

"He did, on more than one occasion," the captain said, smiling at her. "And they held to the story you asked them to tell him. That they were one of the few families who adhered to the Ischia tradition that once a wedding date was set, the future bride and groom should not lay eyes on each other until the rehearsal dinner the night before the wedding."

"A sly one like Bartoli might question such a tradition," Nonna Maria said. "But his earlier marriage was in Northern Italy, and there they tend not to be as superstitious as the ones living near the tip of the boot."

"While he might be suspicious, he won't be able to go near the money unless he gets Anna to marry him," Captain Murino said. "That should be enough for him to hold his powder."

"Was any of the family's land included?" Nonna Maria asked.

"Five acres," Captain Murino said. "The land the family has was inherited. And, as you know, they sublet the land to wine growers in the area. That, plus the money Anna has in the bank, was incentive enough to keep Bartoli in check."

"But no papers were signed," Nonna Maria said.

"None were offered and Bartoli knew enough not to ask," the captain said. "He took them at their word."

"And Anna's trust stays in her name after she is married?" Nonna Maria asked. "For as long as she lives?"

"That is the agreement," the captain said. "Did you convince Anna to do her part in your little scheme?"

"I asked her to help me, much as I have tried to help her," Nonna Maria said. "I told her Bartoli was a dangerous man and, if she helped us, she would prevent him from harming other innocent young women. She's a brave girl and agreed to do what I asked."

"I will allow your plan to play out, Nonna Maria," the captain said. His mood had grown dark and serious, ignoring for the moment the loud applause and the spectacle of the fireworks. "I will help you set the trap to snare Bartoli. But once that is in motion and we have proof in our hands of his past deeds, Bartoli falls to me."

"I care only that no harm comes to Anna or her family," Nonna Maria said. "The crimes committed by Bartoli are a carabinieri matter. Once he is exposed, he belongs to you."

"I promise you, he will pay for what he has done, Nonna Maria," Captain Murino said. "With a long prison sentence or with his life. It makes little difference to me which path he ultimately chooses."

Nonna Maria looked at the captain and nodded. They then both turned their attention to the festivities that surrounded them.

37.

NONNA MARIA SLOWLY made her way along the candlelit corridors of the basement, the thick stone walls cold and wet to the touch. The terra-cotta floor was damp from mildew and slippery in places. She turned one final corner and saw two young men standing on either side of a wooden door, a long-discarded piece of an old sailing vessel. She waited as the man closest to her turned and unlatched the door and swung it open. Then she moved past him and walked into the lit and cold wine cellar.

The door behind her closed and latched. Nonna Maria looked at the rows of wine bottles, each nestled comfortably inside its allotted slot. She had never seen a wine cellar so large and with such a vast collection of bottles, each labeled with year and vintage. Ignoring the chill she felt in the temperature-controlled room, she maneuvered down the well-lit halls toward a small circular wine-barrel table. Two large oak chairs straddled the sides of the table and two large candles rested in the center, next to two empty wineglasses and an open bottle of Biondi-Santi.

Nonna Maria walked up to the table and waited, hearing footsteps headed in her direction from the opposite end of the massive cellar. A tall, heavyset man in his mid-fifties soon came around one corner and stopped in front of the table. Before he spoke, he reached for the bottle of Biondi-Santi and filled each of the wineglasses.

"I thought this would be the best place for us to sit and talk," the man said. "I took it as a given that a woman as formidable as you and one capable enough to set a meeting with someone like me would enjoy a good glass of wine."

The man handed Nonna Maria a glass and then raised one in his hand. "To your health," he said. "And to mine, now that we're at it."

They both took a sip of the Brunello and placed their glasses back on the table. "I agreed to meet with you out of curiosity, if nothing else," the man said. "I've heard quite a deal about you. And I thought it best to take your measure with my own eyes."

The man was Cesare Monte, and he was the head of the Camorra, the most feared organized-crime organization in Naples and the surrounding areas. He had taken over the crime ring first run by his grandfather and then his father and was thought to be the most ruthless gangster in Southern Italy. He had a rich head of dark hair, graying at the temples, and a salt-and-pepper beard, evenly trimmed. He was dressed in gray slacks and a button-down black shirt and wore a thin Armani leather jacket.

"I hope I won't disappoint you," Nonna Maria said. "If so, then it would have been a waste of your time as well as mine."

"It depends," Monte said. "On what it is you came to ask of me."

"You vacation in Ischia every summer," Nonna Maria said. "Along with your wife and children. And before you, your father did the same, brought you to the island when you were just a boy."

Monte sipped his wine and nodded. "I understand you knew my father," he said. "You either helped him with a problem or he helped you. I never did get the full story on how you two connected, only that your paths had crossed."

"And that should stay where it is," Nonna Maria said. "Between me and your father."

"I wasn't asking," Monte said.

"In the years your grandfather and then your father ran their business, they never brought trouble to Ischia," Nonna Maria said. "And in the few years you have been in charge, neither have you. Not until now."

"What is your definition of trouble?" Monte asked.

"Drugs," Nonna Maria said. "I know about the gambling and the moneylending, that hasn't changed since the Greeks ruled the island. But, until this year, drugs were never part of it. But they are now."

Monte lowered his glass and sat in one of the oak chairs. He gestured for Nonna Maria to do the same. "What kind of drugs are we talking about?"

"I'm not an expert on drugs," Nonna Maria said. "But from what I've been told, it's cocaine. And it's being sold in large batches throughout the island to both tourists and locals. And, sooner or later, that can bring trouble to your door. Trouble you don't want or need."

"From you?" Monte asked.

"I'm an old woman," Nonna Maria said. "There's very little I can do to a man like you."

"From who, then?" Monte asked.

"The tourists who visit Ischia usually come from wealthy families," Nonna Maria said. "If a family member of theirs gets caught with the drugs or, even worse, takes more than he should and there is a tragedy, they will not go away without a struggle."

Monte nodded and took another sip of his wine.

"Then you have the local carabinieri to consider," Nonna Maria said. "I know that a man in your profession and at your level doesn't worry about them, but the ones stationed in Ischia are sent there for one purpose only—to make sure the summer season moves along without issues. And drugs, at least the kind being distributed now, will eventually cause a problem. For them and for you."

Monte refilled his glass, keeping his gaze focused on Nonna Maria. "Let me stop you there," he said. "I'm not moving cocaine, heroin, or any drug that could cause issues on Ischia. And it's not because I'm a saint or because I'm not aware of the profit to be made moving that kind of supply. Neither my grandfather nor my father wanted it brought to the island, and it was their wish I not deal in it, either. So I haven't. I kept my word to them to this day."

"I know," Nonna Maria said. "And for that you have my respect. But someone is moving drugs on Ischia, and because of that a good friend of mine is dead."

"And you know who these people moving the drugs are?"

"I haven't set eyes on them," Nonna Maria said. "But I know a young man who does. He owes these men money, and they are having him work off his debt by moving drugs from his boat to the island. In return, they take the money the drugs bring in and slowly reduce the money he owes."

"And your friend got in their way," Monte said.

"Yes," Nonna Maria said. "It was his boat they were using to move the drugs. My friend's death has been called an accident, and I'm sure these men will start shipping drugs to the island again as soon as they can. Once again, using the first mate as their . . . as their . . . I'm not sure I know the term that is used."

Monte smiled. "Middleman," he said.

"I am willing to pay off the young man's debts," Nonna Maria said. "But I don't want to give money to the two men shipping the drugs."

"Who do you want to give it to?"

"To you," Nonna Maria said. "A man in your position knows how to clean up debts such as the one the young man has accumulated and help clear him out of his current situation."

"And why have you picked me as your middleman?"

"Because I'm trusting you," Nonna Maria said. "Your father was a man of his word. I expect no less of his son."

Monte finished off his glass of wine and walked around the table and stood next to Nonna Maria. "I'll make sure your money will be used to pay the young man's debts," he said to her. "But I have a feeling you knew I would do that even before you came here to meet me. So is there something else you want me to do? Another favor you need from me?"

"There is," Nonna Maria said. "But I never ask for more than anyone is willing to give."

"I will clear the two men moving drugs to Ischia from your table," Monte asked. "Since they have done business without approval from me."

"I have other plans for them," Nonna Maria said.

"Such as?"

"They must be arrested for the murder of my friend," Nonna Maria said. "Stand trial and be sentenced to prison."

"That can't be done without a witness," Monte said. "And the young man with the debt can't risk being the one to point them out as the killers. He was on that boat and would be arrested as an accessory."

"The young man was there," Nonna Maria said. "He did his best to help prevent the crime from taking place. Which makes him one of the two witnesses to what happened."

"Two witnesses?" Monte said. "Who else was on that boat?"

"My friend's dog," Nonna Maria said.

Monte laughed and patted Nonna Maria's hand. "You have spine, old woman," he said. "I not only admire that, I respect it. I don't know how you will get the dog to point the finger at the two men, but I'm sure you'll figure a way."

Nonna Maria shrugged. "The dog doesn't need to talk to mark the men as guilty," she said.

"Until they are apprehended, the two men in question could bring harm to you or members of your family," Monte said. "I can make sure nothing like that happens."

"I've already made arrangements in that area," Nonna Maria said. "Through another old friend."

"Il Presidente," Monte said. "I heard he might be out and about again. But you know better than anyone that he's been out of commission for a long time. In his day, there were few better. But many years have passed since then, and he might be a bit rusty."

"He's a desperate man in need of one more chance," Nonna Maria said. "And the two he's tracking don't have the skills to match up against his, rust or not."

"In that case, we have ourselves a deal," Monte said. "There will be no drugs moved to Ischia. And the young man's debts will disappear as if they never existed. Now, as to that second favor?"

"I need help with a man named Andrea Bartoli," Nonna Maria said. "I'm certain that's not his real name. But he is set to marry a local girl, which, in my mind, puts her in danger."

"You're capable enough to stop a wedding from taking place," Monte said. "You don't need my help in that regard."

"You're right," Nonna Maria said. "I don't. Not for that."

"For what, then?"

"Bartoli murdered a woman in Florence a few years back," Nonna Maria said. "His wife at the time. The carabinieri there ruled it an accident."

"Which you don't believe," Monte said. "Or why else call it a murder?"

"The car she drove had been doctored enough to cause it to flip over and burn," Nonna Maria said. "And I know Bartoli had the damage to the car done or did it himself."

"But you can't connect him to it," Monte said. "You need proof it was him."

Nonna Maria nodded. "A man in your business must, on occasion, cross paths with men like Bartoli. You know how they work and who they work with. That is the second favor I come to ask."

"You're right, old woman, I have seen far too many men like Bartoli in my life," Monte said. "I have four daughters of my own, and I make sure no one like this man ever comes near them. They're grifters, always on the hunt for the easy score. Even if that score leaves behind a family in mourning."

"Bartoli may be working with a partner," Nonna Maria said. "I can't say for certain if it's a man or a woman. But if I had to stake blood on it, I would say he works with a woman."

"What makes you so sure his partner is a woman?" Monte asked.

"In most cases, women are smarter," Nonna Maria said, "and think things through before they act. They're not impulsive. I'm going by observation more than personal experience."

Monte stared at Nonna Maria for a moment and nodded. "My father respected you, and I can see why," he said. "Men like this Bartoli travel in small circles. It won't take me long to find you the proof you need. I'll get word to you soon as I know."

"Other than to thank you, I have no way to return the favors you are doing for me," Nonna Maria said.

Monte smiled. "I'll be on the island with my family early next month for a few weeks," he said. "Maybe I can come by your home, and we can sit and have a coffee together. When my father spoke about you, he always mentioned how much he loved your coffee. Do you still make it as well as you once did?"

Nonna Maria returned the smile. "The older I get, the stronger I make it," she said.

"Then you will have done me a favor," Monte said. "One I will always cherish."

Nonna Maria rose from her chair and turned to walk out of the wine cellar.

"Before you go," Monte said to her, "take any bottle you want off the rack. My gift to you."

Nonna Maria looked back and smiled at Monte. "I will take one, but not for me," she said. "My parish priest loves a good bottle of wine. I will gift it to him but not tell him where it came from."

"A woman who knows how to keep a secret," Monte said. "I'm liking you more and more, old woman."

38.

ANNA SAT IN the third row of the empty Santuario del Soccorso in the borough of Forio. The picturesque church, dating back to the fourteenth century, is encased in all-white plaster and faces out to the sea, making it one of the most scenic houses of worship in Europe. Inside, the numerous votive offerings feature notes and prayers that span decades, by sailors, visitors, immigrants, and those in need of healing miracles from the saints lining the walls.

Anna looked up when she saw the shadow of a man approaching from the side of the church. She held her breath until he drew closer and she recognized the familiar face.

"I didn't mean to startle you," Captain Murino said. He paused to genuflect and make the sign of the cross before standing and sliding into the pew next to Anna. "I parked a distance away and walked," he said. "Thought it best neither one of us be seen."

"Does the pastor of the church know we're here?"

"He does," Captain Murino said. "He's out front, pretending to enjoy the view and smoke his afternoon cigar. He'll keep an eye out for any strangers who may pass by. I also have cars stationed at both roads that would lead a driver here. So you can relax. No one will harm you while you're here."

"I'm nervous and frightened, Captain," Anna said. As she spoke, Murino couldn't help but notice how young and frail the girl appeared. These ordeals weighed heavier on the victim than they did on anyone else, and he could see that the strain had left its mark. "I hope I can be brave enough to do what Nonna Maria has asked of me. I would like nothing more than to see Bartoli brought to the end he deserves."

"You are brave, Anna," Captain Murino said. "And both Nonna Maria and I have complete faith in you. You may not be the first woman lured into Bartoli's trap, but you are helping to make sure you will be the last. This game he has chosen to play with the lives of others must come to an end."

"You think he suspects a trap is being set for him by you and Nonna Maria?" she asked.

"He's a suspicious man by nature," the captain said. "As he should be, given the life he leads. But he'll go through with it. Men like Bartoli always believe they are smarter than the ones chasing them. And that error in judgment is what ultimately leads to their downfall."

Anna turned away from the altar and looked at the captain. "You've gone after men like him before?"

Captain Murino nodded. "Sadly, yes," he said. "What happened to you has happened to many innocent young women. How it happens varies from region to region and from city to city. Men like Bartoli have a set of skills to draw a woman in and make her believe his love is genuine. Anyone can fall prey to such a scam."

"If the plan you and Nonna Maria have come up with works, what will happen to Bartoli?" Anna asked.

"It depends," the captain said. "If we link him to one of his past crimes, that will be enough to arrest him and send him to trial."

"If not, he will be free to go?"

"Not necessarily," Captain Murino said. "I can come up with charges to hold him—from endangerment to blackmail. But that is not what I will use to put him where he belongs."

"How will you do that?" Anna asked.

"I believe Bartoli is guilty of murder," the captain said. "A murder committed against a young innocent woman much like yourself. One who fell victim to his charms and paid for it with her life."

Anna's face reflected the shock she felt. Her hands began to shake and she swallowed hard before she spoke. "Was this woman someone you knew?" she managed to ask, her voice echoing off the alabaster walls of the empty church.

The captain turned and stared at Anna for several moments, then slowly nodded his head. "I not only knew her," he said, his voice as cloaked with emotion as Anna's was with fear, "I loved her. I have no doubt Andrea Bartoli is responsible for the death of my sister. I will do everything and anything in my power to see he gets the justice he deserves. How that justice is meted out—with his trial or his funeral—matters very little to me."

39.

LUIGI BEPPO AND Angelo Narini shoved Buonopana against the side of a large pine tree and held him there. They were in the middle of the Giardino degli Aranci, now empty in the early afternoon. "What do you want from me?" Buonopana managed to utter, sweat and saliva meeting at the corner of his lips, his upper body visibly shaking.

"We need you to start moving the shipments and we need to start tonight," Beppo said. "Either pay the money you owe or start moving our drugs back onto the island."

"And if I don't?" Buonopana asked. "If I refuse? Will you kill me, too? And what will that get you? You won't be able to move your drugs and you won't have your money."

"You're not the only one on this island with a boat and a mountain of debts," Beppo said. "It won't take long to find someone else eager to take your place."

"And, even better, we rid ourselves of you once and for all," Narini said. "That's once you pay off your debt, of course."

"His debts have been paid off," Nonna Maria said. "In full."

She stepped out from behind the shade of a thick grouping of pine trees and stood several feet away from the trio.

"You're the old woman who sticks her nose in our business," Beppo said. "And here you are again, where you shouldn't be."

"I've been coming to this park since I was young," Nonna Maria said. "It's open to anyone who lives on the island or, in your case, visits."

"You said his debts have been paid off," Narini said, pointing a finger at Buonopana. "You're wrong, old woman. None of what he owes has found its way into our pockets."

"It's not in your pockets," Nonna Maria said. "The money is in the hands of Cesare Monte. As far as he's concerned, the debts have been cleared."

Beppo and Narini stared at Nonna Maria for a moment, attempting to connect the old woman standing in front of them with the Camorra crime boss from Naples. "How do we know what you say is true?" Beppo asked. "How would someone like you even get close to a man like Monte?"

"That should be of no concern to you," Nonna Maria said. "All that should matter is that Buonopana's debts are clear."

"Even if what you say is true, we're not ready to walk from this, old woman," Narini said. "We have business with this young man, and we intend to continue going about it."

"Your business on Ischia is finished," Nonna Maria said. "And your time here is over. You'll soon be arrested and charged with the murder of my friend Pasquale. And if the court finds you guilty, you will spend the next twenty years looking at the bay from a Naples prison cell."

Beppo laughed. "You believe this old woman?" he said. "Shooting off her mouth like that. And without anything to back up her talk. No proof. No witnesses."

"You must enjoy being on the wrong end of life," Nonna Maria said. "I have everything I need for the carabinieri to bring you in and charge you with the crimes you are guilty of—murder and selling drugs."

"And where is this proof of yours, old woman?" Beppo asked, moving away from Buonopana and toward Nonna Maria. "If you have it, show it to us."

Il Presidente came up behind the two men and stood next to Buonopana. He moved in silence, barely kicking up dust as he inched his way toward them. He looked at Buonopana. "Did you get it all on tape?" he asked him.

Buonopana nodded. Beppo and Narini turned at the sound of the man's voice and stood gazing at the large figure standing over them, massive and menacing. "Who the hell are you?" Beppo managed to blurt out.

"A nature lover," Il Presidente said.

Narini glared at Buonopana. "I should have killed you along with the old man, got rid of you both the same night," he said.

He lunged for Buonopana but was stopped short by a quick and solid right hand from Il Presidente. The hard blow landed in the center of Narini's chest and sent him sprawling to the ground, gasping for air. Il Presidente then shifted his attention to Beppo. He grabbed him by the collar of his black T-shirt and tossed him against the side of a pine tree. He watched him fall to the ground, blood flowing from his nose and mouth.

Nonna Maria moved closer to the two fallen men. "Our proof is in the wire young Buonopana was brave enough to wear," she said. "That, along with the testimony he will give about your drug-running business in return for no charges brought against him. That's proof and one of our witnesses."

Nonna Maria looked at Il Presidente and nodded. The big man reached behind a thick pine tree, bent down, and lifted Pippo in his arms. He turned and lowered the dog, who walked between Beppo and Narini. Pippo began barking and growling and scratching at the two men, forcing both to cover their faces against the onslaught of the small dog.

"And there's our second witness," Nonna Maria said. "Pasquale's best friend."

"You're mad, old woman," Narini gasped. "Nothing you have will hold up in court. Our lawyers will rip your case to shreds."

"Maybe," Nonna Maria said. "But if that were to happen, you would be handed off to another judge. One much harsher than any you will meet in a court of law."

Beppo and Narini glared up at Nonna Maria. "Cesare Monte doesn't need a confession on a wire or a small dog who misses his owner to find you guilty," she said. "And whatever punishment he chooses will be much worse than two decades in a Naples jail."

The sirens of the carabinieri could be heard coming off the main road of the port and turning down the side street toward the Giardino. "You should go now," Nonna Maria said to Il Presidente. "Your work here is done."

She then turned to Buonopana, still standing with his back to a tree. "You know what you need to do?"

Buonopana nodded. "Tell the truth," he said. "It's what I should have done from the very first."

Nonna Maria bent down, picked up Pippo, and held him close to her chest. She gazed at both Beppo and Narini. "It looks like our work here is done as well," she said. "Captain Murino will take it from here."

Nonna Maria and Pippo began to walk down the incline, their bodies cooled by the thick overhead branches of the pine trees that covered the Giardino. She smiled as the dog nuzzled against her neck and licked the side of her face. "You are a good dog, Pippo," she said. "Pasquale would have been very proud of you today."

Behind Nonna Maria, the footsteps of the carabinieri approached, and she turned to see them circling Beppo and Narini. Captain Murino was looking down the incline at her. He waved, gave her a smile, and nodded his thanks.

Nonna Maria returned the smile and then continued the slow walk back to her home, eager to put a bowl of water out for Pippo and a fresh pot of espresso on the stove.

40.

"YOU MEAN IT, Nonna?" Gian Luca said, squealing with excitement. "We can keep him?"

"Pippo needs a home," Nonna Maria said to her grandson, "and you've taken excellent care of him. Fernanda is too sick to give him the time and attention he needs and was happy to hear that Pasquale's dog was in good and safe hands. He'll be a good friend to you and you to him. And Il Presidente agrees with me. But from time to time bring Pippo to see him. That would help make a lonely man happy."

"And Mama and Papa?" Gian Luca asked. "Have you told them?"

"I talked to them," Nonna Maria said. "We came to an understanding."

"Does that mean they said yes?"

"I didn't give them time to say no." Nonna Maria smiled. "And they knew keeping Pippo would make you happy. And you keeping him would make me even happier."

"Thank you, Nonna," Gian Luca said. He reached out his arms and wrapped them around her waist, holding her tight. "I love you as much as I love Pippo."

Nonna Maria returned the hug and held on to the boy for a moment. "So, now you need to keep your end of the bargain."

Gian Luca released his hold on Nonna Maria and took a few steps back. "What do you mean?" he asked.

"Sometimes, Gian Luca, in life, you have to give something in order to get something you want," Nonna Maria said. "The something you wanted was Pippo, and that is what you now have."

"And what is it that I need to give?" Gian Luca asked, his words a mixture of apprehension and suspicion.

"You need to look after yourself more," Nonna Maria said. "You leave your room a mess, they tell me, and never help with the dishes. You're not a baby anymore, Gian Luca, and you can't act as if you are. The way you have taken care of Pippo these last few days shows me you can be someone who can be trusted with responsibility. And now your mama and papa are adding on to those responsibilities. I leave it to you to decide."

Gian Luca stayed silent for a moment. Pippo was shuffling between the two of them, brushing his coat against the sides of their legs. "Okay, Nonna," he said. "I'll take care of Pippo, keep my room clean, and help around the house."

"I'm happy to hear that," Nonna Maria said. "Especially since I already told them that you agreed to hold up your end of the bargain."

"What made you so sure I would say yes?"

"One of the benefits that comes with old age," Nonna Maria said. "Plus, I have seen with my own eyes how much you love Pippo, and I gambled you would do whatever your parents asked in return for keeping him."

"Wait," Gian Luca said. "Did you talk to them about buying his food and any medicines he might need? And paying for the doctor when he's sick?"

"That's the final piece of the bargain I made," Nonna Maria said. "I will take care of any costs for Pippo, from food to doctors to medicine. I'll give you a sum each week that should cover food and treats. The vet, Marcello, is an old family friend. His father was also a vet and used to take care of your grandfather's sheep. I'll have him send his bills to me."

Gian Luca fought the urge to cry—to no avail. The tears starting to flow down the sides of his cheeks. They were not tears of sadness but of a young boy's joy. "I'll pay you back, Nonna," he said. "I promise. I'll pay back every euro."

Nonna Maria pulled a clean tissue from the front of her apron pocket and folded it in her right hand. She bent over and wiped the tears from the boy's face. "You have already paid me back in more ways than you can possibly know, Gian Luca," Nonna Maria said.

"How?"

"By taking care of Pippo," Nonna Maria said. "He once belonged to a friend of mine who loved him as a son. And now he belongs to you, and you will love him as a brother. That is worth more to me than any amount of money you can put in my hands. No, grandson, you don't owe me anything. I am the one who owes you."

41.

NONNA MARIA SAT in a cloth chair on the lower deck of the Coast Guard cutter docked in the harbor, a short walk from her home. Across from her was a young officer, his white uniform crisp, his shoes polished to a shine. His name was Antonio Florido, and he was the youngest of the Coast Guard officers assigned to keep the harbor area and the sea beyond safe. He was also one of Nonna Maria's numerous nephews.

"You loved these waters since you were old enough to walk," Nonna Maria said. "Swam in them as soon as you learned how. And you always stopped to stare at the Coast Guard boats that would dock here overnight."

"I even got to ride in some of them when I was a boy," Antonio said. "Depending on who was in charge that day."

Antonio was in his late twenties, and he had an easy manner to go with his quick smile and calm disposition. He was tanned from his many hours out at sea, and it further highlighted his good looks, topped by unruly strands of thick black hair. Despite the outward calm, he had proven to be not one to be trifled with. Last year alone, he captured three speedboats of black marketeers and brought in a disorganized crew attempting to steal one of the many private luxury boats docked outside the port.

Nonna Maria reached into her black bag and brought out a large package wrapped in brown paper. "I brought some lunch for you to have later," she said. "I packed some of your favorites, and I didn't forget to add extra basil and red onion to the tomato salad."

"Grazie, Zia," Antonio said, smiling at Nonna Maria. "It looks like you packed enough to eat for a week."

"Share it with some of the others in your crew," Nonna Maria said. "The more you eat, the less I have to hear your mother tell me how you're wasting away to nothing because of the long hours you work."

"I've heard it, too," Antonio said. "She never thought we ate enough, me and my brothers and sisters. Even though I can't remember a time when I didn't have a meal. Sometimes more than one. I would eat at home, then come visit you and eat again. I'm lucky I don't look like a sumo wrestler."

Nonna Maria smiled. "She was born a worrier," she said. "You can't change that, so you learn to live with it."

Antonio placed the package near the instrument panel and turned back to Nonna Maria. "I know better than to offer you a coffee that wasn't prepared by you," he said. "And I know you don't drink water, and it's still a little too early for a glass of wine. So, I don't know what I can offer you."

"I don't need anything to drink, Antonio," Nonna Maria said. "I need a favor."

"Name it," Antonio said. "If I can do it, it will be done."

"There's a rehearsal dinner in two days," Nonna Maria said. "To celebrate the wedding this weekend between Anna and this man Andrea Bartoli. And, if what I have been told by your mother is correct, you're on duty that night, monitoring who comes in and out of the harbor."

Antonio nodded. "It will be my first night in charge of the watch," he said. "I'll have all six of our boats under my command."

"And you have the authority to stop and search any boat coming in and out of the port?" Nonna Maria asked.

"For any reason," Antonio said. "Though I expect the evening watch to be less hectic than it is during the day. There isn't much activity once the sun goes down."

"Good," Nonna Maria said. "The fewer boats going in and out, the better for what I need you to do."

"You sound worried," Antonio said, resting a hand on Nonna Maria's right arm.

"I only worry when there's a need to be worried," Nonna Maria said. "And on that night, there is a need."

"What is it?"

"I have concerns that Bartoli is planning to do something to Anna on the night of the dinner," Nonna Maria said. "He is a desperate man who knows there are many eyes looking his way. And he is an evil man, and such men can feel a trap about to close in. He may look to move her off the island before the wedding and force her to marry him in Naples or in one of the nearby villages."

"And you want me and my men to make sure Bartoli does not leave the island," Antonio said. "Alone or with Anna."

Nonna Maria nodded. "It's always helpful to make your way through the dark when you have bright lights around you."

"If he attempts to leave the island by boat, he will be caught," Antonio said. "And we'll hold him overnight or until Captain Murino asks to have him released in his custody."

"If he has Anna, you can hold him for kidnapping," Nonna Maria said. "Is that correct?"

"If she tells us she is being taken against her will," Antonio said, "then that will be the charge."

"And if he's traveling alone?" Nonna Maria asked. "Leaving the island as anyone else is free to do? What can you do then?"

Antonio smiled. "This is Ischia," he said. "Not all our laws are written in books. I'm sure once we have him in custody, we'll come up with a reason to hold him."

Nonna Maria returned the smile. She stood, hugged her nephew, and started to make her way off the Coast Guard boat. "You've learned your lessons well," she said. "You'll make a fine commander one day."

"I learned the only way there is to learn," Antonio said, waving as she walked down the short gangplank back onto solid ground. "From the best."

42.

NONNA MARIA STOOD in the back room of Nino's restaurant. There was a long wooden table in the center of the large room, twenty-two chairs lined up on both sides, with a large floral arrangement in the center of the table. The settings were in place, from plates to silverware, and a second large wooden table rested in a corner of the room, topped with a series of buffet trays. A bar was set up next to a stairwell, and a makeshift stage had been put in place for the musicians to play during the dinner.

"So, Nonna Maria," Nino said, his thick arms spread out, "what do you think of the setup?"

"Bravo, Nino," Nonna Maria said with a smile. "I can think of no better place to hold a rehearsal dinner than in your restaurant. You will have helped make it a night to remember."

"Do you want to go over the menu?"

"There's no need," Nonna Maria said. "You and your wife are both excellent cooks. It will be a feast, no matter what it is you have chosen to serve."

Nonna Maria walked toward the bar and glanced at the stairwell curved behind it. "Where does that take you?" she asked Nino.

"To the storage attic," he said. "It's where we keep our supplies—mostly pasta, dough, spices, things of that nature."

"Is there a way out from there?"

Nino nodded. "There is a door that leads out to a rooftop garden," he said. "The staff take their breaks there, have a coffee, smoke a cigarette. I even thought of one day expanding and putting tables there during the summer season. On clear nights, you can see Capri to the right and Vesuvius to the left. Beautiful view."

"Can you get down from there without going back through the storage attic?" Nonna Maria asked.

"Yes, there is a narrow staircase that takes you to the back of the restaurant," Nino said. "From there, you can make your way to the port or to Ischia Ponte, depending on which direction you choose to go."

"Is that the only way out of the restaurant?" Nonna Maria asked. "Other than the front door?"

"There is a third," Nino said. "A side door near the restrooms. It's not used much, but you come out into a small alley, jammed between my place and Arturo's next door, and can make your way to the port that way if you choose. But most of the patrons come in through the front and leave the same way."

"That seems the best way to leave if you didn't want to be seen leaving," Nonna Maria said. "Get up to use the bathroom and then make your way out. It would be a while before anyone noticed you were missing."

"Why are you asking these questions, Nonna Maria?" Nino asked. "Do you think the guests will all be looking to escape without being seen?"

"Not all, Nino," Nonna Maria said. "Just two of them."

"Do you know which two?"

"I have my suspicions, Nino," Nonna Maria said. "But for now, let's leave it as just that."

"If you want, I can have one of the busboys keep an eye on the back door," Nino said. "See which of the guests decide to leave before we bring out the cake."

Nonna Maria shook her head. "There's no need," she said. "I don't want to do anything that will interfere with their plans."

"So you want these two to leave the dinner before it ends?"

Nonna Maria nodded. "If it happens—and there is no guarantee it will—it will prevent a bigger tragedy from happening this weekend."

"The wedding, you mean," Nino said. "Between our Anna and this stranger. You don't think it will happen?"

"Doesn't matter what I *think*," Nonna Maria said. "It only matters what *happens*."

"If I can help in any way, Nonna Maria," Nino said, "no hesitation. I will be by your side."

"Plan your feast and enjoy the evening you have planned so well," Nonna Maria said. "For now, that's all you or anyone else can do."

"You do have a plan in place, then?" Nino said. "To prevent what you most fear will happen?"

"I always have a plan, Nino," Nonna Maria said.

43.

CAPTAIN MURINO SAT next to Nonna Maria on the stone bench in front of Saint Peter's Church. Between them, she placed a sealed manila envelope. For a few silent moments, they sat and watched the tourists and locals walking past, heading for tour buses and boats or to spend another morning soaking up the warm sun on one of Ischia's numerous beaches.

"You were right, Captain," Nonna Maria said. "Your sister did not die in an accident. Her car was tampered with. That is what caused her death. Not the rain or her poor driving. I am sad to tell you she died as you believed. All the proof you need is in the envelope."

Captain Murino lowered his head and nodded. "Finally, I can nail that bastard."

"There's more," Nonna Maria said.

"Tell me," Captain Murino said.

"Bartoli did not doctor the car alone," Nonna Maria said. "He had help. A cousin of his named Carlo Ruffino. In return, Carlo was promised half of your sister's life-insurance money."

"And did he get the money?"

Nonna Maria shook her head. "Bartoli disappeared soon after he collected on your sister's policy," she said.

"Leaving Ruffino with nothing," Captain Murino said.

"Nothing but a desire for revenge," Nonna Maria said.

"And where is this Ruffino now?"

"He lives in Naples," Nonna Maria said. "His address is in the envelope along with a photo. It shouldn't be difficult for the local carabinieri to locate him."

"And you think he will admit to helping Bartoli doctor my sister's car, leading to her death?" Captain Murino asked.

Nonna Maria stayed silent for a moment. "He has more to fear if he doesn't tell you the truth," she said.

"I have learned, Nonna Maria, that men like Ruffino don't fear prison," the captain said. "It is a price they expect to pay for the life they have chosen to lead."

"That may be true, Captain," Nonna Maria said, "but what he fears has nothing to do with a life behind the bars of a prison cell."

"The only fear worse would be death," Captain Murino said.

"Ruffino is in Naples, Captain," Nonna Maria said. "In that city, as you well know, a darker hand determines a man's eventual fate. You are correct that someone like Ruffino does not fear the law or many years in prison. But he does fear the one who truly controls that city. No judge, no jury, no higher power, can help him if he does not do as he is asked. He will stand against Bartoli, believe me."

Captain Murino looked at Nonna Maria for several moments. "You never fail to amaze," the captain said.

"There's another name in that envelope that will be of help to you," Nonna Maria said. "It's the name of Bartoli's primary partner. Her name is Silvana Cerbone. She's the one who helps to choose his targets."

"Do you know where she is now?"

"She, too, lives in Naples," Nonna Maria said. "In an apartment not far from the port."

"And she will agree to testify?" Captain Murino asked.

"She will do as she is told," Nonna Maria said. "Both Ruffino and this woman have done their work without the knowledge and permission of someone who now will decide whether they live or die."

"The Camorra crime boss," Captain Murino said. "A career criminal who should himself be in prison."

"He's a career criminal to you, Captain," replied Nonna Maria. "To me, he is simply the son of an old friend."

"And did this son of an old friend have a hand in helping gather the information you have in that envelope?" Captain Murino asked.

Nonna Maria smiled. "A good friend is always there to help in any way he can," she said.

They sat quietly for several moments, content to stare at the parade of passing tourists and locals. The sky was clear and the sun warm on their arms and faces, and they found comfort in the calm.

"So, what happens now?" Nonna Maria asked.

"We will follow procedure," the captain said. "There will be a formal request to reopen the investigation of my sister's accident. The information in the envelope you've given me will be more than enough to allow us to bring in Ruffino and Cerbone and question them. In the meantime, I can detain Bartoli for suspicion of murder."

"Bartoli will certainly try to tell a different story," Nonna Maria said. "A cornered rat is at its most dangerous. He has the ability to charm. That may not be of any help to him outside a courtroom, but inside, it might prove a strength."

"I won't allow him to walk away," the captain said. "I'll kill him with my own hands, if it comes to that."

"What if there was a second charge against him?" Nonna Maria asked. "One that would not be difficult to prove, even to the most doubting eyes?"

"Such as?" Captain Murino asked.

"What if he were to take Anna away, against her will?" Nonna Maria said. "And what if she would be willing to testify against him once he's caught? I would imagine she would make a much more believable witness than two criminals like Ruffino and Cerbone."

Captain Murino nodded. "A strong witness always makes for a strong case," he said. "But based on just the information in this envelope, I can hold him on suspicion of murder."

"What if you could have him on both crimes?" Nonna Maria asked. "Murder and kidnapping? And with Anna prepared to point the finger at him. Plus, you would have a number of people who would swear they saw Bartoli take away his victim by force. Would that not help ensure a long prison sentence for a man who deserves nothing less?"

"Without a doubt," the captain said. "It would strengthen the prosecutor's case on both counts. While Bartoli might avoid a conviction on one of the charges, it would be difficult for him to walk away a free man from both."

"In that case, why arrest him now?" Nonna Maria asked. "Why not wait until he makes his next wrong move?"

"And what makes you certain Bartoli will make another wrong move?" the captain asked. He turned toward Nonna Maria, his face a mix of curiosity and certainty.

"You're the carabiniere, maybe you can tell me," Nonna Maria said. "Don't men like Bartoli have a habit of making more than one wrong move?"

"And I suppose you already know what that next move will be," the captain said.

"If I said yes, would that not make me a possible suspect?" Nonna Maria asked.

"I have my doubts that even the most seasoned prosecutor could get you to admit to anything that would cause trouble for you or any of your close allies, Nonna Maria," the captain said.

"Being old helps," Nonna Maria said. "People tend to believe the words of an old woman."

"Whatever it is that you may or may not be planning to do," the captain said, "be aware that all such plans, no matter how carefully thought out, contain an element of risk."

"The greater the risk, the better the plan," Nonna Maria said. "And if I did have a plan to corner Bartoli, it would have to be a great one in order for it to work."

"So, the rehearsal dinner goes forward as scheduled?" the captain asked.

"Nino's prepared a feast," Nonna Maria said. "It would be a shame to let all that great food go to waste. I even asked him to put aside a few platters for you and your men."

"Will you be at the dinner?" the captain asked.

Nonna Maria nodded. "But not for long," she said. "I'll stay just long enough for Bartoli to see me. Then I'll leave and come find you."

"Find me?" the captain said, his words unable to hide the surprise behind them. "I'm not going to the rehearsal dinner. There is no reason for me to be there. I'll have some of my men nearby, in case there are issues between Anna's family and Bartoli."

"I know," Nonna Maria said, standing and brushing off the back of her black dress. "But it would be a big help if you were also somewhere nearby, close to Nino's restaurant."

"And tell me, Nonna Maria, what need could you have for me at a rehearsal dinner?" the captain asked.

"You want to capture Bartoli and put him in one of your cells?" Nonna Maria asked.

"More than anything," the captain said.

"In that case, I'll see you near Nino's," Nonna Maria said. "I'll find you and bring you a warm coffee in case there's a cool night breeze."

Nonna Maria nodded her goodbye to Captain Murino and then turned down the sloping hill, past the side of the church, making her way back to the only home she had ever known.

44.

ANNA STARED AT the foamy waves slamming against the shiny black rocks that encased the half-mile beach property in front of Da Salvatore's restaurant. She sat at one of the corner tables, shaded by a thick umbrella, her hands folded around a large cappuccino. She turned and looked over at Nonna Maria, sitting across from her. In the distance, Luca had dropped anchor on his boat and had gone below to work on the engine.

"Why do you think Bartoli will want me to go with him tonight?" Anna asked. "The wedding is not far off. Why not wait until we're married, when I would have no choice but to go with him? Why lead him to believe the wedding will not happen?"

"Because we can't risk waiting for the wedding day, and neither can Bartoli," Nonna Maria said. "Men like Bartoli have a way of sensing when trouble is closing in. He would want to stay one step ahead of that. Taking you with him tonight will be his first move. Especially when he hears what you have to tell him."

"That my parents want to delay the wedding yet again," Anna said.

Nonna Maria nodded. "They want to be sure he is the man for you," she said. "The man you will be spending the rest of your life with."

"And you are sure he won't be able to get off the island?" Anna asked. "Because if he does, I'm lost to all of you."

"The Coast Guard will see to that," Nonna Maria said. "They will be checking every boat coming in and out of the port. They will have their lights and their eyes on any boat that so much as moves."

"So, then where do you think he'll take me?" Anna asked.

"If he can't get you off the island, he'll look for a safe place to hide," Nonna Maria said. "That would mean heading up to the top of the island. It's an easy place to keep you hidden. Until he decides on his next move."

"I'm scared, Nonna Maria," Anna said.

"I am, too," Nonna Maria said. "And Bartoli is counting on us being too afraid to do anything to stop him. He has never had a reason to fear any woman, especially one so young and one so old. This is our chance to make him pay for all the wrongs he has committed. Let him think what he thinks. It will work to our advantage."

"And you and the carabinieri will be following us?" Anna asked.

"Like a cat after a mouse," Nonna Maria said. "Every step of the way. My steps, of course, will be a bit slower than the others."

Anna lifted the cappuccino cup and took two long sips, then placed it back on the table. Nonna Maria reached out and put one hand on Anna's wrist and gave it a gentle squeeze. "You are not alone in this," she said. "You haven't been since the day you came to me and asked for help."

Anna smiled at Nonna Maria and nodded. "I'll go along with your plan," she said. "And then follow Bartoli wherever he leads me. I've caused enough problems for the people who care about me and love me. Getting involved with Bartoli was my mistake, and now it's time to correct it."

"After tonight," Nonna Maria said, "you will never have to concern yourself with Bartoli again. As the years pass, his name will be nothing more than an unpleasant memory."

Anna grasped Nonna Maria's hand and turned her gaze once again to the waves splashing against the long line of black rocks. "I believe you, Nonna Maria," she said. "With all my heart, I believe you."

45.

IT WAS A hot and humid night, without the usual breeze off the waters of the bay, as was often the case when the summer season neared its height. To make the guests feel more comfortable, Nino had his staff turn on the overhead ceiling fans, keeping them on low speed, aware of the superstitious beliefs of some of the older guests. "I would even have put some large fans in the four corners of the room," Nino told Nonna Maria earlier in the evening, "but then I would be blamed for every sore throat, cough, and cold caused by the cool air coming at them from all sides."

"And you would have to leave a scarf and a sweater on every chair," Nonna Maria said, "to protect them from the draft. It's better the way you have it. And it's supposed to be hot and humid this time of year. They have their hand fans and their wine and water. That will be all they need to get them through the night."

The guests began to arrive at seven, Bartoli one of the first. He was dressed in tan slacks, a starched white shirt, and a light-blue blazer. He went straight to the bar and ordered a glass of chilled white wine and a glass of sparkling water. He leaned on the counter and watched as the guests came in, not bothering to introduce himself to anyone.

Anna arrived closer to seven-thirty. She was dressed in a sleeveless blue dress and black flats. Her hair was parted in the middle and rested against both sides of her face. Her parents were by her side. Her mother, a thin woman in her late forties with thick brown hair and a tanned, unlined face, seemed nervous and apprehensive. Her husband, older by at least a decade, wore an ill-fitting suit and wiped at his brow with a folded handkerchief. He was bald and slightly overweight but seemed pleased to be surrounded by familiar faces.

Bartoli walked over to Anna and handed her a glass of wine. She turned to her parents and handed the wineglass to her mother. "I only drink water," she said.

"That will change," Bartoli said. "Once you are my wife, you will be freer to do as you wish."

Nonna Maria came up behind them. "She has always been free to do as she wishes," she said to Bartoli. "And she is free to drink water. Just as I am free never to drink water."

Bartoli turned to Nonna Maria. He had a smile on his face, but his eyes betrayed the anger raging within. "I didn't expect you to be here," he said. "I didn't think you cared much for parties."

"I like them as much as I like to drink water, which is to say not at all," Nonna Maria said. "But there's always an exception. Especially if it involves a special young lady and a family I've known for many decades."

"Then you must be in a festive mood," Bartoli said. "To see this young lady settle down with a man she loves."

Behind them, waiters were rushing from kitchen to table, placing large platters of food in the center and walking around with appetizers and offering them to the guests.

"I will be," Nonna Maria said, "when that day comes. But until then, there is food to be enjoyed and wine to be savored."

"But that special day is only hours away," Bartoli said.

"At my age, we count time in minutes, Bartoli," Nonna Maria said. "Not in days or hours. And I've learned that even within those minutes, there is so much that can change. From a thought to a life, it all can be turned upside down in a matter of just one minute."

"You bring darkness to an occasion that should be filled with light and happiness," Bartoli said.

"It's a dark world," Nonna Maria said. "As you yourself know so well."

"But sometimes you must allow some light to shine in," Bartoli said. "And this night, this very special night, is one of those times. I'm sure even you and I can agree on that."

Nonna Maria looked around the large space, packed now with friends and relatives of Anna and her family, eating, drinking, and a few even dancing to the old Ischia love songs played by the three-piece band in the far corner of the room. Then she turned back to Bartoli. "It is a special night in so many ways," she said to him. "A night that will be remembered."

Nonna Maria saw Anna standing next to her mother in the center of the room. She caught her eye and without another word to Bartoli walked toward the young woman.

"I can't stop my hands from shaking, Nonna Maria," Anna said in a low voice, careful not to be overheard by those around her, searching out Bartoli, aware of his every move and with whom he stopped to speak.

"Rest easy," Nonna Maria said, rubbing Anna's arms with her thick, gnarled hands. "And follow our plan. As soon as you have a moment alone with him, tell him your parents do not wish the wedding to move forward. Once he hears that, I am confident, Bartoli will try to steal you away."

"And you'll find me once he does," Anna said. She shivered despite the warmth of the crowded room.

"I promised you, little one," Nonna Maria said, nodding her head. "And I never break a promise. Dishes and cups on more than one occasion. But a promise? Never."

46.

"WHAT ARE YOU saying to me, Anna?" Bartoli asked her. They were standing in a long corridor, the men's restroom on their right, the ladies' on their left. Behind them, the room was a loud and festive mix of laughter, music, and conversation.

"My parents want to delay the wedding again," she said, working up the strength to bring conviction and believability to her every word. "They need more time."

"Time for what?" Bartoli demanded to know. His anger was now rising to a full boil, his face red, and his hands gripped Anna's arms so firmly they would for certain leave behind a mark.

"For them to get to know you," Anna managed to say. "And for them to be sure that we both are in love and that we're not getting married for any other reason."

"What other reason can there be?" Bartoli said. "If they don't believe I love you now, what makes you think they will feel any other way in a week or a month or even a year? They are a foolish old pair if they think that to be the case, and you are an even more foolish young girl if you believe it, as well."

"They are no different than any other parents," Anna said. "They want to be certain we're making the right decision for all the right reasons."

Bartoli brought Anna closer to him, holding her tight to his chest, his lips next to her right ear. "Listen to me," he whispered. "You and I are to be married, and no one can stop that from happening. Not your parents. Not that foolish old woman who follows me like a shadow. Not even the captain of the carabinieri. No one. Do you understand what I'm telling you?"

Anna was trembling and could only manage to nod her head.

"In a church on this island or in a civil ceremony in Naples, it makes no difference to me," Bartoli said. "You and I will be wed, and we will live our lives far removed from this place."

"I don't want to leave my family," Anna said, unable to stop the tears that were flowing down her cheeks.

"I *am* your family," Bartoli said into her ear. "From here on, we are a family of two. And there is no need for you to get permission from your parents to do anything. The only one you need to ask is me. I decide for you, from this moment on."

Bartoli pushed Anna away from him but held his grip on her arms. "Have I made myself clear?" he asked.

Again, Anna nodded.

"You would have no life with these people you only think love you," Bartoli said. "Your future is now where it belongs. With me."

Anna nodded once more, and Bartoli released his firm grip

on her arms. "We should get back to the party," she said, wiping the tears from her eyes and face.

"The party's over," Bartoli said.

He grabbed Anna by the hand and led her down the corridor to the thick wood door that led to an alley outside the restaurant.

47.

THE FIAT 500 sped up the sinuous curves of the paved roads leading out of the port and into the highest reaches of the island. Bartoli was behind the wheel, moving at a high speed, wheels squealing on every sharp turn, the car tilting against the hard angles of the narrow road. Anna sat next to him, her seatbelt secure, both her hands grasping on to the edges of her seat. "Where are you taking me?" she asked, as the Fiat zoomed past the outer borough of Barano and continued its upward climb.

"A place where we can be alone," Bartoli said. "It will be empty and quiet this time of night, and no one will bother us. We can hide there for a few days and then, when things quiet down, we can make our way off this damn island and start our new life together."

"How do you know of such a place?" Anna asked in a quiet voice, as curious as she was frightened.

"Since this marriage has taken forever to happen and you were nowhere to be found, I had plenty of time to explore the island," Bartoli said. "And during one of those trips, I stumbled upon this place. And I made a note of it—in the event that something might occur to delay this marriage again. And, as expected, it has come to pass."

Bartoli swerved away from a divider, the Fiat hitting a curve at too fast a clip, the rear wheels turning furiously, the smell of burned rubber in the air. He held on to the steering wheel with both hands, sweat forming on his forehead and streaming down the sides of his face.

"My family will never stop looking for me," Anna said. She was looking out her window, the port area now melding with the view of the harbor and the bay, the night lights stretched as far as she could see. The sky above was dark and clear, filled with an array of stars that seemed to sparkle.

"Let them waste their time," Bartoli said, shifting gears and forcing the engine to grind even harder, every turn up the winding road a potential death trap. "As soon as we are off this island, you will be a mere memory to them."

"What was it you put in my gelato?" Anna asked. "That first day we met. What did you give me?"

Bartoli laughed as he steered the car off the paved road and onto a gravel one, spitting dust and small rocks in his wake. "What makes you think I put anything in your gelato?" he asked with a smirk.

"Because I know you did," Anna said. "I don't remember anything that happened to me for weeks after eating the gelato you brought me. You didn't have one. You were drinking iced espresso. I felt as if I were in a dream, and when I woke up I found myself engaged to you, a man I barely knew let alone loved."

Bartoli slowed the car as it inched up a sharp incline, the road now narrower, surrounded on both sides by thick rows of grapes in full bloom. "I was on the hydrofoil coming over from Naples. I overheard these two women behind me talk about a special potion that makes people act in ways they would not normally act. They mentioned relatives they had who were in unhappy marriages all because years earlier they had been given either a drink or food with this powder mixed in."

"Did they tell you where you could get this powder?" Anna asked.

Bartoli shook his head. "I never asked," he said. "But I knew on an island like Ischia, where superstitions thrive for centuries, it wouldn't take long to not only learn more about the powder but also where I could get my hands on a packet."

"What made you sure it would work?" Anna asked. Her fear had begun to dissipate, replaced more by interest in the events that had conspired to place her in the company of a man she was convinced was a danger to her and her family. "And that it would work on me?"

"I wasn't sure," Bartoli said, navigating a tight turn around one of the olive groves as he ventured farther up the sloping side of what seemed to be a large vineyard. "But if it was going to work, it had to be on someone young and impressionable. A description that fit you perfectly."

"Whatever it was, it clouded my mind enough that I fool-ishly agreed to marry a man I didn't love," Anna said.

"Have you really convinced yourself it was some powder in your gelato that made you behave the way you did?" Bartoli asked.

"What other reason could there be?" Anna asked. "It was La Fattura that made me agree to marry you."

"Believe what you choose to believe," Bartoli said. "It's much more acceptable, especially on an island like Ischia. Everyone is so quick to blame a secret potion for someone's behavior rather than for them to confront the truth."

"And what is the truth?" Anna asked.

"I gave you attention," Bartoli said. "A sense of excitement. You became infatuated. I was your chance to escape from this island to live a life in places you would only be able to dream of. It wasn't any magical powder, Anna. It was me and what I would be able to offer you."

"I love my life here," Anna said. "My family and my friends are here. Ischia is where I belong."

Bartoli smiled. "Yes, it's beautiful, safe, and packed with tourists in the summer. But what kind of life will you have? You will live with your family until you meet a local, settle down, have a family, and live a life much like your parents'. I offered you a chance to escape that. And you reached for it. Then you panicked and blamed it on a powder I put in your gelato."

"You did put something in it," Anna said in a loud voice.

"Yes, I used the powder I bought," Bartoli said. "But I never believed it would work. And deep in your heart, you know it doesn't, either."

Anna stared at Bartoli for a moment and stayed silent, her face red, her hands and arms coated with a cold sweat. She glanced around, trying to get her bearings, trying to see beyond the thick vines, the tight roads, and the darkness that engulfed them. "We're in the D'Ambra vineyard," she finally said, looking down at the bay and the surrounding lights, which seemed far enough away to be located on another island.

"There's a stone house up ahead," Bartoli said. "I noticed it when I came here to tour the vineyard and taste their wines. It's at the highest point of the island. It's not a place that has many visitors. Most of the people who live on Ischia don't even know it's here."

"What about those who work the vines?" Anna asked. "They'll be sure to see us and ask why we're here."

"No one other than the owner of the vineyard goes into the house," Bartoli said. "And he is rarely there. You learn quite a bit on a tour if you pay attention and ask the right questions. So, not to worry. You and I will finally be together and alone."

Bartoli made a sharp right turn and parked the car under a thick row of overhanging trees. He waited as Anna got out, then stepped from behind the wheel and grabbed armfuls of discarded vines and tossed them on top of the car, keeping it hidden from view.

Anna stood off to the side, watching him, shivering in the cool night air. The temperature in the vineyard, located in the borough of Serrara Fontana, was at least fifteen degrees cooler than it had been at the port and would only grow colder throughout the night. Bartoli stood back, checked the car one final time, and then turned to Anna, reaching out a hand for her to take.

"It's up there, just beyond the edge of that small hill," he said, pointing a finger into the blanket of darkness.

Anna recoiled from Bartoli's touch. "I'm not going up there with you," she said. "I'm not going anywhere with you. This is as far as I am willing to go. You can walk up that hill, but you will be doing it alone."

Bartoli leaned in closer to Anna. "I have wasted enough time," he said, his voice filled with a rage she had never heard from him before. "You can spend the night with me in the stone house—or be tossed off the side of this mountain, through the vines and to your death. It is up to you."

Anna glared at Bartoli and then with both hands pushed him away. The shove caught Bartoli off guard, and he lost his footing on the soft ground and fell onto his back, deep into a batch of thick shrubbery. She stared at him in disbelief for a moment, then turned and began to run down a hill.

48.

"STOP THE CAR," Nonna Maria said to Captain Murino. "We need to go the rest of the way on foot."

"If that's the case, you wait in the car," the captain said. "I won't have you walking these steep hills, especially in the dark. It's not safe."

"I've been walking these hills and through these vines since I was a girl," Nonna Maria said. "And I see no reason to stop now. I know these paths better than any of your men do. They'll be going in circles all night without the help of me and some friends."

"First, and with all due respect, you're not a young girl anymore," the captain said. "And second, what friends are you talking about?"

Nonna Maria smiled. "This is a large vineyard, more than forty acres of vines, sloping hills, and rough roads," she said. "And the chances are your men, as capable as they are, have never been up here. So I asked a few of my friends to help us find Bartoli and Anna."

"Where are they now?" the captain asked. "Your friends?"

"They're spread out, each covering a parcel of land and a

section of vines," Nonna Maria said. "Most of them, like me, came up here as children, some to play and some, when times were tough, to work and earn money to help at home. If Bartoli and Anna are to be found, they are the ones who will point us in their direction."

Nonna Maria pointed toward a sloping hill. She rested one hand under the captain's arm, and they began a slow walk down. "What makes you so sure this is where Bartoli would come?"

"It's the safest and quietest place on the island," Nonna Maria said. "Bartoli is sharp enough to know he would be blocked from leaving the island by boat. He had a car, which is the fastest and easiest way to come up here, especially at this hour of the night. And he's taken four tours of the vineyard in the time he's been on the island. One would be enough to tell him about the wine and the history of the winemakers. The other three visits had little to do with wine."

"A car can only get you so far into the vineyard," the captain said. "But once he's on foot, there are dozens of places for him to hide. If not more."

"It would not be wise for him to spend the night on the sloping sides of the vineyards." The voice came from behind them, and the captain turned as soon as he heard it. "They would both wake up soaked from the heavy dew of the morning."

Nonna Maria smiled at the sound of the voice and looked up at the massive man standing behind her. It was Il Presidente.

"How long have you been up here?" she asked.

"Since late afternoon," he said, nodding a hello to Captain Murino. "A few of the others came up with me, about half a dozen in all. I even convinced Pepe the Painter to leave his post for one night."

"Where are they?" the captain asked.

"They're scattered through the hills," Il Presidente said. "Just to make sure Bartoli isn't hiding under any piles of vines and shrubs. But most likely he's heading toward the stone house or somewhere close to it."

Captain Murino pulled a radio off the right lapel of his uniform and alerted the men he had scattered throughout the property that there were others in their midst, also searching for Bartoli. He then turned to Nonna Maria. "Where is this house located?"

"At the highest point of the vineyard," Nonna Maria said. "It's built into a side of the mountain. A perfect place to escape the hot and humid air of summer."

"And the carabinieri," Il Presidente said with a smile. "I should know. As Nonna Maria could tell you, I used it a few times in years past myself to avoid being captured."

"I'll pretend I didn't hear that," the captain said.

"It would be for the best," Nonna Maria said. "The past is not a concern now. Bartoli and Anna are who we came to get."

Captain Murino turned to Il Presidente and nodded. "Lead the way," he said. "I'll have my men follow us as best they can. I'll station two of them farther down the path, in the event Bartoli gets past us."

"Our friends have been told to stay spread out and to listen for any movement they might see or hear," Il Presidente said.

"Not to worry, Captain," Nonna Maria said, catching the look of concern on Murino's face. "They will not attempt to capture Bartoli on their own or to do anything that might bring harm to Anna. But your men will know if and when they have spotted him."

"How will they alert us?" the captain asked.

"There are roped-off cords of kindling wood placed along many of the paths," Il Presidente said. "Doesn't take more than a match to light them. That will be a signal to your men."

"Is there a way down from the other side of the house?" the captain asked. "On the other end of the mountain?"

"Yes," Il Presidente said. "But that path does not lead to escape. It leads to death."

49.

ANNA STUMBLED AND rolled down a sharp incline, scraping her right knee on a shorn tree limb and gashing her left elbow against the edge of a rock. She lay still for a moment, gazing out into the blanket of darkness, doing her best to figure out how far she was from a main access road. She thought she had heard movement on each side of her as she ran down the sloping hills, convincing herself that it was nothing more than packs of wild rabbits and stray dogs rummaging among the foliage.

She got back to her feet, her right knee more of a concern than her elbow, forcing her to slow her run to a fast walk. She looked to her right and saw the lights of the faraway harbor, dimmer now in the hours when darkness ruled. She was both frightened and confused, unsure if she was heading in a direction that would bring her closer to safety and fearful that Bartoli would reappear at any moment and drag her away.

She had been to the vineyard only once before, for a daytime visit with her parents several years ago, so she was on foreign terrain. She jumped at the sight and sound of two rabbits rummaging through a stack of thick, discarded vines. She was weary and couldn't stop trembling, out of fear, tension, and the evening chill. All she could be sure of was that the farther down she went, the brighter the lights of the harbor began to appear, and the closer she might be to finding someone to come to her aid.

There were no homes around that she could see and no lights to guide her. The path was steep and the curves sharp and she walked with caution, careful not to fall again against any rocks or tip over the side of an incline into a ravine below. Each passing minute felt like an hour, and a dreaded thought infiltrated Anna's mind, one she couldn't shake, no matter how much she tried. She began to believe she would not make it through this long, torturous night alive, and if that were indeed the case, she had no one to blame but herself.

Anna stopped and leaned closer to the ground. She crouched down and glanced to her left. There was a rustling among the vines and the unmistakable sound of heavy footsteps heading toward her. She looked frantically in every direction, seeking a place where she could hide. But she was too frightened to move, frozen in place, her arms shaking, and her legs felt as if there were weights attached to them. She managed to lie facedown in the dirt path.

She saw a man's boots emerge from the rustling of the vines. He walked slowly, then bent down and reached out a hand for her to take. "Anna," he said, his face and body shrouded in darkness. "Anna, it is me—Luca. We have come here to get you and bring you back home."

Anna looked up, took Luca's hand, and then wrapped her arms around his shoulders. He gently lifted her to her feet and they both stood, holding each other, nuzzled together in the middle of a dark, dirt road. "How did you know where to find me?" she said.

"I didn't," Luca said. "Nonna Maria and Captain Murino did. They were the ones who came up here to rescue you and to capture Bartoli."

"Where are they?" she asked, fear and anxiety rushing out of her, quickly replaced by curiosity and questions.

"Spread out across the vineyard and the hillsides," Luca said. "Many of Nonna's friends came to help in the search, and the carabinieri are out in force, as well."

"Have they found Bartoli yet?" Anna asked.

"I'm not sure," Luca said. "The cell service here comes and goes, depending on where you're positioned. Last I heard they were still searching."

"Call them if you can," Anna said. "Let them know you found me and that Bartoli is heading for the stone house at the top of the vineyard."

"How did you manage to get away?"

"I pushed him, and he lost his footing and fell into a batch of vines and twigs," Anna said. "Then I started to make my way down the hills, hoping to find someone to help me."

"Well, then, your journey was a success," Luca said, easing Anna from his chest and giving her a wide smile. "You found me, and I will help you."

Luca pulled a cell phone from the back pocket of his jeans and checked the signal. "I have one bar," he said. "Let's hope it's enough."

"You can put your phone away, Luca," Captain Murino said, coming up around the curve behind them. "I've already alerted my men and some of the others. A few of them will be here soon with a blanket and some water for you, Anna. And then one of my men will take you down to where we left our cars. You'll be safe and warm there."

"Thank you, Captain," Anna said. "And you, Luca. I still can't believe you came and found me."

Captain Murino walked up to Anna and rested a hand on her arm. "There is one person you must thank above all," he said to her. "And I'm pretty certain you know who I'm talking about."

"Nonna Maria," Anna said with a smile. "Is she with you?"

"Where else would I be at this hour?" Nonna Maria said. She was sitting on a low stone wall, catching her breath, her large black bag against the side of one leg, a thick black shawl wrapped around her shoulders. "The good captain looked like he could use some company on his search."

Anna ran from the captain's side and rushed to Nonna Maria. She wrapped her arms around the older woman and held her tight. "I am sorry to have caused you so much trouble," she said.

"I'm happy to see you are back in safe hands," Nonna Maria said. "And I never miss a chance to come to the vineyard. The night air is good for my health, or so I've been told. And to be surrounded by rows of grapes a few weeks away from being picked and turned into wine always lightens my heart."

A young carabinieri officer arrived, a blanket folded across one arm and a large bottle of water held in his right hand. "My car is parked a short distance away," he said to Anna, her arms still wrapped around Nonna Maria. "It's not a far walk. You can sit there and rest."

"Are you coming with me?" Anna asked Nonna Maria, releasing her hold.

Nonna Maria shook her head. "Not yet," she said, picking up her handbag and standing. "There's still one more piece we need to put in place. This is not over. Not until Bartoli is captured and in the hands of the carabinieri. And I want to be there to see it happen."

"Be careful, Nonna Maria," Anna said, watching as the older woman began her slow walk toward Captain Murino. "Please be careful."

"Children need to be careful," Nonna Maria said over her shoulder. "The old need to be wise."

50.

CAPTAIN MURINO STOOD in the middle of the steep incline, less than twenty feet from the entrance of the single-structure stone house. One carabinieri officer had made it through the thick brush and was closing in on the house from the front, and a second had managed to crawl his way through the rocks and small boulders that framed the house, standing now above the entrance.

A short distance away, Nonna Maria was making her way up a narrow path, thick vines brushing her face and arms, her sandals slipping on slick white rocks and mounds of soil.

"It's over, Bartoli," the captain said. "Come on out and give yourself up."

"You plan on arresting me?" Bartoli said from inside the stone house. "On what charge?"

"We'll start with trespassing," the captain said. "But then we'll toss in kidnapping, and that makes the rope a bit tighter. And then we'll add the murder of my sister to complete the picture."

"You live in a dream world, Captain Murino," Bartoli said. "I'll admit to trespassing. But that only brings with it a small fine. Nothing more."

"Perhaps," Captain Murino said. "But kidnapping is a serious offense. If convicted, that will put you away for as much as ten years."

"It would be hard to convince a court I kidnapped my own fiancée," Bartoli said. "We simply wanted time away from the crowds of the port. To spend time alone together."

"She'll tell a different tale, Bartoli," Captain Murino said. "One that the court will believe. Then add to that the charge of murder and you will face the only life you truly deserve—one spent behind prison bars."

"You need to believe your own eyes, Captain," Bartoli said. "Your sister died in an accident. It was investigated and there were no charges filed, as you well know. You continue to pursue these baseless accusations and I will be the one forced to take legal action."

Nonna Maria slipped and fell to her knees, cutting her right foot against the side of a white rock. She reached for one of the vines and lifted herself back up. She was a dozen feet away from the front of the house. She eased her way farther up the hill, looking for a path she used to take when she was a child visiting the vineyard with her family. A path that led to the side of the house, now entangled in vines and old fig trees. A path that would let her reach Bartoli from behind.

"I'm not the only one who believes it was murder, Bartoli," Captain Murino said. "Your friends Carlo Ruffino and Silvana Cerbone seem to think so as well. And I'm certain they will testify to the events that led to my sister's death."

Bartoli remained silent for a moment. "They would never go

against me," he finally said. "They know the price paid for such a betrayal."

"They will want to save their own skin," Captain Murino said. "You were the one who betrayed them, especially Ruffino. You kept the insurance money for yourself. But none of that matters to him or to the woman. What does matter is what will happen to them if they don't testify against you."

"They won't fear the carabinieri or a prison sentence," Bartoli said. "And as far as money is concerned, I'll make it right with Ruffino."

"You're right, Bartoli," Captain Murino said. "Ruffino and Cerbone aren't afraid of me or of doing prison time. But they do fear what awaits if they don't stand against you."

"And what would that be?" Bartoli asked.

"Whether Ruffino and Cerbone live, die, or spend their days in prison won't be decided by the carabinieri or by any judge," Captain Murino said. "Their fate belongs to their master. Perhaps even yours, as well. The streets of Naples will be their judge and jury. That is why their only recourse is to testify and bring you to an end."

"You still have to take me in," he said.

"Nothing will give me more pleasure," the captain said. He snapped open the button on his holster and rested a hand on his gun.

Nonna Maria was now standing with her back to the cold stone wall of the small house. She was a few feet from the entrance. Her foot was bleeding and she had long scratch marks on both of her arms; there was a line of blood across her right cheek.

Bartoli stepped out of the house. Nonna Maria moved closer and pushed Bartoli from behind, sending the taller, stronger man to his knees.

Bartoli turned and saw Nonna Maria standing over him. He glared at her for a moment and then jumped to his feet and grabbed her with both hands. "I had a feeling you would be here," he said.

"I go where I belong," Nonna Maria said. "And tonight it is here, to see you taken away."

Bartoli turned Nonna Maria around and shoved her in front of him, his right arm wrapped tight around her waist. He grabbed at the collar of her dress with his free hand. "That might have happened, old woman," he said to her. "But with you now by my side, the carabinieri would not risk causing you any harm. Who would think you of all people would be my good-luck charm?"

"A rabbit's foot is a good-luck charm," Nonna Maria said. "Not an old woman."

Bartoli pulled his hand away from Nonna Maria's collar and wrapped his elbow around her throat, clutching tight, forcing her to gasp for air. "Let's see which way the good captain wants this to play out," Bartoli said. "Me in handcuffs or you lying dead by my feet."

51.

CAPTAIN MURINO REACHED the top of the hill and was standing several feet across from Bartoli and Nonna Maria. "Let her go," the captain said, his semiautomatic held in his right hand.

"The old woman is my shield, Captain," Bartoli said. "One wrong move and I will snap her neck and be rid of her for good."

Captain Murino stayed silent for a moment, his eyes focused on Nonna Maria. "You harm her and I will empty my gun in you," he said to Bartoli.

"Don't concern yourself with me, Captain," Nonna Maria said. "Do what needs to be done."

Bartoli tightened his grip around Nonna Maria's neck, making it difficult for her to catch her breath. "A little tighter and all your worries will be over, old woman," Bartoli whispered in her ear.

"I have no worries," Nonna Maria said.

She slowly eased her hand against her dress and then reached for the cut on the side of her face. She slid her fingers up to her hair and twisted her body in an attempt to be free of Bartoli's grip.

"Stay still, old woman," he said. "I can hold you up dead just as easily as I can alive."

Nonna Maria's right hand was now grazing Bartoli's arm and

touching the back of her thick white hair. "You're hurting me," she managed to say.

"And that brings a smile to my face," Bartoli said.

Nonna Maria's fingers rested on the right side of her hair, held in place by a series of thick black hairpins. She slowly pulled one of the pins out and brought her arm back down to her side, her fingers wrapped around the pin, sharp end pointing out. She braced her feet and slightly turned her body a few inches away from Bartoli. "Move again, old woman," he said, "and it will be the last movement you make."

Captain Murino had eased a few steps closer, looking for an opening to advance on Bartoli. Behind them, Il Presidente was silently making his way toward Bartoli and Nonna Maria.

Nonna Maria bent her legs, ignoring the pain it caused her right hip, lifted the sharp end of the hairpin, and slammed it down into Bartoli's thigh. It went through his pants and punctured the skin.

Bartoli released Nonna Maria, sending her skidding to the ground, facedown in the dirt. Captain Murino raced toward them. Bartoli pulled the hairpin out of his thigh, a line of blood starting to stain his pants. He looked down at Nonna Maria.

Bartoli lifted a leg and was preparing to kick the back of Nonna Maria's head, when he was grabbed from behind by Il Presidente, who lifted him off his feet and shoved him toward Captain Murino. Il Presidente bent to Nonna Maria and helped her to her feet. "Are you okay, Nonna Maria?" he asked, wiping the dirt from her face.

Nonna Maria gave him a warm and welcome smile. "I could use a glass of wine," she said.

52.

CAPTAIN MURINO STOOD across from Bartoli. He was holding his weapon with both hands, right index finger resting on the trigger, a slight pull away from bringing an end to the man who had killed his sister. Around him, his men also had their weapons drawn.

He looked at Nonna Maria standing next to Il Presidente and gave her a quick smile, then turned back to Bartoli. "You never seem to tire of harming women," he said to him. "But your time for that has come to its end."

Nonna Maria stepped away from Il Presidente and stood next to the captain. "Men like Bartoli never fear a bullet," she said in a low voice.

"He deserves to die, Nonna Maria," Captain Murino said.

"He deserves punishment," Nonna Maria said. "Let him spend his days and nights where he belongs. In a prison cell."

"He will still be alive," Captain Murino said. "While my sister rots in her grave. There is no justice in that."

"The easy choice would be to shoot him," Nonna Maria said. "But all it would do is allow him to ruin one more life. And I know you won't let that happen."

"What makes you so certain, Nonna Maria?" Captain Murino said.

"Because you're the better man," Nonna Maria said.

Captain Murino stayed silent for a few moments, glaring at Bartoli. He then lowered his weapon and signaled to his men. "Take him into custody," he said to them.

"Not just yet," Il Presidente said, raising a hand to keep the carabinieri officers in their place.

Il Presidente stepped up closer to Bartoli, stared at him, lifted his right fist, and landed a hard blow against the side of Bartoli's face, sending him crashing through a row of thick vines. He glared down at Bartoli. "That's for Nonna Maria," he said to the stunned and fallen man.

Then he turned back to Captain Murino. "Now you can have him," he said.

Il Presidente reached out and hugged Nonna Maria and then made his way down the sloping hill, disappearing into the darkness.

53.

TWO CARABINIERI OFFICERS lifted Bartoli from the ground, cuffed his hands at his back, and started to walk him down the incline. Bartoli glared at Nonna Maria as he passed her, still dazed from Il Presidente's blow.

"Looks like you got what you wanted, old woman," he said to her.

"And you got what you deserved," Nonna Maria said.

She watched as Bartoli was led away. Captain Murino and Nonna Maria followed them down the incline and made their way past a cluster of Nonna Maria's friends who had come to help her in the search for Anna and Bartoli.

Standing in a large circle were Pepe the Painter; Gabriella from Naturischia; Gaspare from La Dolce Sosta; Don Marco from the parish; Mario from the tour-bus company; Aldo from the Bar Calise; Susanna from the port; Nonna Maria's grown children and their spouses; Nino from the restaurant; Silvio Rumore, the captain of the *Princess;* her grandson Gian Luca with his dog, Pippo, by his side; and Sara D'Ambra, one of the owners of the vineyard.

Captain Murino eased in alongside Nonna Maria. "You went

above and beyond tonight," he said. "I should be angry with you for putting yourself in such danger. And I should also thank you for all that you've done."

Sara stepped forward, embraced Nonna Maria, and then turned to the assembled group. "You have all worked hard tonight and done well," she said. "What better way to celebrate than to head down to the cantinas and enjoy a few bottles of wine?"

The group nodded and applauded. They turned and began to make their way down the sloping, curving paths to the cantinas. Nonna Maria watched as they left, talking and laughing.

"You should go with them, Nonna Maria," Captain Murino said. "No one deserves a glass of wine more than you."

"And what about you, Captain?" she asked.

"I should get back and start filling out the paperwork with the various charges against Bartoli," he said. "Besides, they are your family and friends, and you should celebrate with them."

"They are your friends now, too, Captain," Nonna Maria said. "As you are mine. And as much as I enjoy a nice cold glass of wine, I enjoy it even more when I drink it with a friend."

Captain Murino put out his arm and Nonna Maria held it tight with her left hand. Together, they began the slow descent, neither one speaking, each one finding comfort in the quiet of a dark night.

54.

NONNA MARIA WALKED next to Giovanni Buonopana on the far edges of the port, heading toward his docked boat. It was early on a warm and seasonal day; a small group of tourists were gathered by a café, enjoying a morning coffee and some pastries. It had been a week since the arrest of Bartoli and Anna's return to her family, and while Nonna Maria no longer had any cases she felt required her help, she still had unfinished business that needed her attention.

"I'm happy it turned out well for you," said Nonna Maria. "And I hope you've put your gambling issues behind you."

"I have, Nonna Maria, believe me," Buonopana said.

"How many months' probation did they give you?" she asked.

"Six, starting this week," Buonopana said. "I report to the carabinieri once a month and, if I stay out of trouble, my record will be cleared once the six months are up."

"Then what you need to do is simple," Nonna Maria said. "Don't gamble and never borrow from people you don't know."

"I spoke to Pasquale's widow," Buonopana said. "She will get half of what I earn from working the tour boat. It won't make up for her loss, but it's the least I could do, given the hurt I caused."

"It was a gesture from your heart," Nonna Maria said. "Those are always remembered."

"I worry about the two who murdered Pasquale and came after me for the money I owed," Buonopana said, his voice and manner reflecting the concern he felt. "I'm not a brave man, Nonna Maria. I won't be able to fight them off."

Nonna Maria nodded. "You will never see those men again," she said.

"What makes you so sure?"

"They chose a life that doesn't end well for those who enter it," Nonna Maria said. "And they moved drugs into Ischia without the permission of the man who controls their destiny. They made their choice. He made his."

Buonopana looked out at the waters of the bay. "I would have liked to see them standing in front of a magistrate, charged with his murder."

"You would have been part of the trial if that had happened," Nonna Maria said.

They were now standing alongside the *Lucia Bianca*, the boat Buonopana had taken over from Pasquale. "What happened to them could have happened to me," he said.

"You learned a harsh lesson at a young age," Nonna Maria said. "I have little doubt you will lead a good life, one that would make Pasquale proud. Keep my old friend in your heart. Let him be your guide."

Buonopana reached out and embraced Nonna Maria, holding her close for a moment. She gazed up at him and smiled.

"There is one thing you need to do," she said. "It would be a favor to me and to Pasquale."

"Anything you ask," Buonopana said.

"Get yourself a dog," Nonna Maria said. "He'll be a good friend to you as Pippo was to Pasquale. And in this world, we all could use a good friend."

55.

IL PRESIDENTE STOOD at the base of Nonna Maria's house and waited for her as she walked down the spiral stairway. He seemed agitated and wiped thick beads of sweat from his forehead with the back of his right arm.

"I've been thrown out of my room at the port," he said. "It was cleaned out, my things taken away."

"I know," Nonna Maria said. "You don't live there anymore. You live here."

She turned and walked toward a shuttered door on the first floor of her home. She opened the door and turned on a light switch. The room was completely furnished, with bed, chairs, couch, dining table, television, and a fully equipped kitchen.

She stepped into the large, freshly painted room, Il Presidente right behind her. "I can't live here, Nonna Maria," he said. "This is more than I need and much more than I can afford."

"The rent is the same as you were paying for the room at the port," Nonna Maria said. "And you don't need to worry about food. I have a habit of cooking more than one person can eat, so there's plenty for both of us. And you will drink my coffee and share my wine."

"I can't accept this, Nonna Maria," Il Presidente said. "I appreciate it, but I don't take charity from anyone, not even you."

"There is no charity involved," Nonna Maria said. "Look at the outside of this house. It's in need of work, and that's what you'll be doing. My guess is it will take four, maybe five months to get it into proper shape."

"But I know nothing about fixing houses," Il Presidente said.

"Then maybe six to seven months," Nonna Maria said.

"And after that?"

"After that, there's more work," she said. "It's an old house and I'm an old woman. The boiler barely makes it through the winter. The hot-water tank works only when it wants to. And don't get me started on the pipes. Also, I'm not as good with the garden as I once was, so you'll have to take that over for me. Moving in here is not charity. Moving in here is hard work."

Il Presidente looked around the large room and took a deep breath. "Everything here is new," he said.

"There are clothes hanging in the closet and others folded in the bureau," Nonna Maria said. "I hope they fit, but if they don't, bring them to Mario the tailor and he'll adjust them for you."

"Why are you doing this for me?" he asked.

"I'm not doing anything for you," Nonna Maria said. "I'm doing it for me. Look what I get out of it—a house fully repaired, a garden in full bloom, and someone to walk up the hill with me after dinner to sit on the stone bench in front of the church."

"I've been living alone for such a long time," Il Presidente said. "I was made fun of, ignored by most, feared by some. But never by you. I told myself that none of it mattered. But it did. There was no one for me to tell who would care. But you cared, and while I appreciated it, I never understood why."

"That will give us something to talk about as we sit on the stone bench," Nonna Maria said. "For now, you wash up and settle in. I've got a pot of coffee on the stove. Come up if you would like a cup."

Il Presidente looked at her and smiled. "Don't you want to know how I take my coffee?" he asked.

"In this house there is only one way," Nonna Maria said, starting her walk up the stairs and returning the smile. "And that's to drink it the way I serve it."

56.

NONNA MARIA WAS holding two heavy plastic grocery bags as she walked up the steep hill on Corso Vittoria Colonna. She had her black tote bag flung over her right shoulder. She was walking slowly, not helped by the weight and the morning heat, heading for home.

Anna was walking out of a clothing store when she saw Nonna Maria. She rushed up to her side. "Give me the bags," she said to her. "You shouldn't be carrying such heavy items."

"In this weather," Nonna Maria said, "no one should. You take one and I'll take the other. Move my shoulder bag to my free hand. It will keep me balanced."

She handed Anna one of the grocery bags and the two began to walk up the hill. "I'm glad I ran into you," Anna said. "I wanted to talk to you about a few things. And to thank you for your help with all that happened."

"Let's stop and rest by the church," Nonna Maria said. "The shade there will keep us cool."

"Did you believe me when I said Bartoli had me under the spell of La Fattura?" Anna asked.

Nonna Maria smiled. "On this island, most everyone believes in it and all claim to know someone it has happened to," she said, wiping at her brow with a folded handkerchief. "What matters is, did you believe it?"

Anna thought for a moment and then said, "Part of me did. I did feel and act in a different way than I usually do."

"But it wasn't the only reason you agreed to the marriage?"

"No," Anna said. "I was taken with the idea of this handsome stranger falling madly in love with me. What girl my age wouldn't be? He promised a life of adventure, romance, travel. I guess I got caught up in it."

"And now?" Nonna Maria asked.

"I'm back where I belong," Anna said. "And with someone who cares for me and always has."

Nonna Maria smiled. "I'm sure Gennaro is as happy about that as you are," she said. "He's a hardworking young man. I see a bright future for him. You have chosen wisely this time."

Nonna Maria picked up her two bags and waited as Anna picked up her bag, and the two continued their walk toward her home.

"Who is all this food for?" Anna asked.

"You never know who will come through my door and bring with them an appetite," Nonna Maria said. "Besides, other than drinking coffee and wine and being around my family and friends, there's nothing I love more than to spend time in my kitchen and cook meals my mother taught me."

Anna smiled and glanced at Nonna Maria. "You enjoy cooking more than solving crimes?" she asked.

Nonna Maria returned the smile. "I don't solve crimes," she said. "That's what Captain Murino does. I help friends when they are in trouble."

57.

GIAN LUCA WRAPPED the lead on Pippo's leash around his right wrist, smiling as the dog weaved in and out among the passing tourists walking along the Lido. Many of them stopped to take photos and selfies of the view, a widespread vista that, on this warm, clear day, offered a panorama of the bay as well as sightings of Capri, Procida, and, in the distance, a glimpse of Naples.

"They take so many photos," Nonna Maria said, walking alongside her grandson. "But they never stop and enjoy what's in front of their eyes. Make what they see a memory. It is much better to have that, instead of an old photo that will end up tossed in the back of a drawer."

"They keep the photos in their phone, Nonna," Gian Luca said.

"Your father bought me one of those phones," Nonna Maria said. "Told me to call him if I needed anything or if there was an emergency. He said I could listen to music and watch movies on the phone. I don't understand why I need a phone to listen to music, when all I have to do is open my window and hear my neighbor sing the Neapolitan songs I've heard since I was your age. She's got a great voice, better than any voice I can hear over a phone."

"I've been reading these stories about a detective, and they made me think of you," Gian Luca said.

"Why would these stories remind you of me?" Nonna Maria said.

"He takes on cases, like you do, to help people," Gian Luca said.

"Is he on Ischia, this detective?"

Gian Luca smiled. "No, Nonna," he said. "He lived in London, years ago."

"Was he good at helping people?" Nonna Maria asked.

"There was no one better," Gian Luca said. "He always solves his cases. At least the ones I've read. Works with the police. Like you with Captain Murino."

"What is his name?" she asked.

"Sherlock Holmes," Gian Luca said.

"I've heard his name before," Nonna Maria said. "Agostino mentioned him to me."

"Holmes works on his cases with a doctor," Gian Luca said.

"I wonder if that was why Agostino brought up his name," Nonna Maria said. "Maybe he wants to help me if I get involved with helping a friend again."

"Are those the only cases you take, Nonna?" Gian Luca said. "Ones that help your friends?"

"I don't take cases, Gian Luca," Nonna Maria said. "If a friend calls and needs help, I do what I can."

"We could help you," Gian Luca said. "Me and Pippo."

"I can always count on your help," Nonna Maria said. "And

Pippo's. Now, tell me, does this detective, Holmes, work with a dog? And does he have family and friends he can turn to when he needs help?"

"He has a brother, but I don't think they like each other," Gian Luca said.

"That's sad to hear," Nonna Maria said. "He must be a lonely man. He should have left England and come to live in Ischia. He might not have had a lot of cases, but he would have had many friends."

"If you like, I could come and read some of the stories to you," Gian Luca said.

"I would like that," Nonna Maria said. "You read, while I drink my coffee and wine and learn how he solves his cases."

"Sherlock Holmes doesn't drink coffee or wine, Nonna," Gian Luca said. "He drinks tea."

"Then it's a good thing the two of us can never meet," Nonna Maria said. "I can't trust a man who doesn't drink coffee or wine."

58.

AGOSTINO SAT ACROSS the table from Nonna Maria, sorting through his medical bag and pulling out a blood-pressure gauge, an oximeter, and a thermometer. "You look tired," he said to her, giving her a warm smile as he gauged her appearance. "These little adventures are taking a lot out of you, whether you admit it or not."

"Old women always look tired," Nonna Maria said. "And if I'm tired, which I'm not, maybe it's because I followed your orders and am drinking less coffee than I usually do."

"You should go to the beach," he said, ignoring her complaint. "Get some sun, maybe even go for a swim. You live a three-minute walk from one of our most beautiful beaches and yet you never go there."

"It's crowded and noisy," Nonna Maria said. "And I don't own a bathing suit and, at my age, why would I even think of buying one? But I look out at the water when time allows."

"So, you do go to the beach?"

Nonna Maria shook her head. "You don't need to go to the beach to see the water and get some sun," she said. "I go to Da Salvatore, the restaurant that overlooks the bay. I sit there, talk to my old friend, and watch the waves splash against the rocks and let the sun warm my face."

Agostino pushed back his chair and walked over to Nonna Maria. He reached for her right arm and wrapped the blood-pressure monitor around it. "I want you to take it easy," he said, his eyes on the gauge. "From what I hear, you were running all over the island the last couple of weeks."

"That's talk from people who have nothing to do but talk," Nonna Maria said.

Agostino peeled off the blood-pressure cuff, folded it, and rested it on the table. "Your pressure is higher than I would like," he said.

He checked her heart, took her temperature, and then placed her right index finger in the opening of the small oximeter. "That's a new toy," she said. "What does it do?"

"It registers the oxygen level flowing through your blood-stream," he said. "The higher the number, the better the flow. By some small miracle, you're over ninety-five, which is perfect."

"Which means I'm as good as I should be," Nonna Maria said. "Save your worries, Agostino, for your sick patients. They need you more than I do. Now, pack your medical stuff away. It's time to sit and eat."

Within minutes, Nonna Maria had filled her large table with platters of lemon chicken, roasted peppers, marinated eggplant, a tomato, basil, and red onion salad, and a plate filled with mixed olives and chunks of pecorino cheese. "I didn't make pasta," Nonna Maria said, "because I know you try your best not to gain weight. I kept the meal simple. But, in case you change your mind, I have the water boiling and can put in the pasta anytime you want."

"Are you going to sit and eat with me?" Agostino asked, starting to fill his plate.

"You're not the only one who has to keep an eye on his weight," Nonna Maria said. "But I'll sit with you and have a cup of coffee."

"You missed your true calling," Agostino said. "Instead of helping your friends with their troubles, you should have opened a restaurant. If a Michelin critic ever sat at this table and tasted this feast, he would award you three stars."

"He's always welcome," Nonna Maria said. "Stars or no stars."

Nonna Maria drank her coffee and was about to pour herself a second cup when she saw a young woman standing at the entrance to her home. Agostino turned and looked at her, as well. She was in her early twenties, dressed in a yellow sundress, her black hair matted down with sweat, her cheeks red, and her tanned arms glistening with moisture.

"What's wrong, Claudia?" Nonna Maria asked.

The girl was short of breath and spoke in spurts. "My mother sent me to get you, Nonna Maria," she gasped. "Someone came into our home while we were eating lunch. I never saw him before. None of us had."

"What did he want?"

Claudia shook her head, sweat beads falling off her hair. "I'm not sure," she said. "He told us this visit was a warning, the next time we could expect it to be much worse. He kept his hands in his pants pockets and looked at us in a way that made us all frightened."

"Did you call the carabinieri?" Agostino asked.

"No," Claudia said. "My mother told me to run and find Nonna Maria and ask if she would come to the house."

"Tell your mother I'll be there in a few minutes," Nonna Maria said. "And tell her not to worry. We'll figure out who this man is and what it is he wants."

Claudia nodded, turned, and ran down the steps of Nonna Maria's home, back to her own. Nonna Maria got up from the table, reached for her black tote, and placed several items inside the bag.

"Why do we bother having the carabinieri on Ischia?" Agostino said. "If every time someone needs help, they come running to you and not them. I'll never understand it."

Nonna Maria walked briskly into the kitchen and rested several empty Tupperware containers on the table. "I want you to take the leftovers and bring them home to the family," she said to Agostino. "And there's a bag in the kitchen filled with jars of fresh tomato sauce and those stuffed peppers you like. Take that with you, too."

"Did you hear what I said to you a few minutes ago?" Agostino said. "About you relaxing, getting some sun, stop running all over this island? Did any of that register?"

Nonna Maria nodded. "I heard every word, Agostino," she said. "And I promise I will do as you asked. I will relax, get some sun, and even take naps in the early afternoon."

"I didn't ask you to do that," Agostino said. "You've never taken a nap in your life—why start now?"

Nonna Maria smiled. "There's only one reason I can think of," she said. "To make my doctor and my favorite nephew a happy man."

"And when will this all begin?" Agostino asked.

"Soon," Nonna Maria said.

"Be careful," Agostino said. "Please, Zia. That's all I ask. Be careful."

"Old women are always careful, Agostino," Nonna Maria said. "That's how we get to be old women."

Nonna Maria gave him a wave and headed out the door and began the slow walk down the steps of her home.

"I have to go now," she said. "A friend needs my help."

ACKNOWLEDGMENTS

THIS BOOK WOULD not have been possible if it were not for the real Nonna Maria. I wrote about her in my last book, *Three Dreamers,* and out of that grew the idea of turning her into a fictional character helping to solve crimes on her beloved island of Ischia. So, once again, I owe my thanks to an old woman who showed me nothing but love and kindness across seven glorious summers spent in her company.

My editor, Anne Speyer, did her usual terrific work editing this book and, during the journey, treated Nonna Maria with a loving and respectful touch. It is a much better book because of her talents and I am grateful to have her in my corner. And to my Ballantine family—especially Kara Welsh and Jennifer Hershey—thank you for giving me a place to call home all these many years. And the more time passes, the more grateful I am to have Gina Centrello as a publisher and friend. She has always been there for me and always will be.

Jesse Shuman is my wingman—skilled and always at the ready to lend a helping hand. And a heartfelt shout-out to the publicity, marketing, and promotion folks. And to the audio team, led by Dan Zitt, a warm thank-you. It was a pleasure working with you.

I want to thank my many friends in Ischia, an island where I have spent some of my happiest days. I first went there as a boy of fourteen and return every year. We have known each other for decades now, grown old together, and they will always have a special place in my heart. Most especially, I want to thank the real Paolo Murino, more my brother than a cousin, who is one of the kindest and smartest men I know. I hope I have done him justice in making him a proud member of the carabinieri.

A warm embrace to the Keating family—the very definition of what a family should be, loving and being there for one another every day. And my warmest thanks to Vincent, Anthony, and Ida Cerbone of Manducati's; Giuliano and Mario at Primola; the gracious and beautiful Una and the wonderful Mary from Neary's keep a light shining on the legacy of Jimmy Neary, one of the classiest and kindest gentlemen the town has known; Larry Zilavy; Lou Pitt, Jake Bloom, Ralph Brescia, PJ Barry, Stanley Tucci, Hank Gallo; Adriana Trigiani; Lisa Scottoline; Leah Rozen; Dr. Michael Cantor, Dr. George Lombardi, Pete and Carol Barry, Guido and Dorothy Bertucci, Antonio and Branca at the Excelsior in Ischia; Franco, the best driver this side of Mario Andretti; the family at Da Salvatore for the amazing meals and good company; Angela Rumore; Leo Trani; the D'Ambra family, especially the amazing Sara, the best winemaker on the island; Gaspare and Pepe for the years of friendship; and my Zio Mario for seeing what Ischia could be long before anyone else did.

For my two grown children—Kate and Nick—both of whom have grown to love Ischia as much as I have, thank you for always being there and putting up with me and loving me as much as you do. And to my son-in-law, Clem, for being a great dad and a wonderful husband. He is as smart as he is kind.

And, best of all, my heart goes out to the one and only Oliver Lorenzo Wood. I have been told down the years that having a grandson changes your life. I actually never believed it until Oliver came along. I can't imagine loving anyone as much as I do the Little Man who calls me Ba Ba. He has been a great gift to us all and never fails to bring a smile to my face and leave a warm feeling in my heart.

If you enjoyed

NONNA MARIA

and the Case of the Missing Bride,

read on for an exciting preview of
Lorenzo Carcaterra's next Nonna Maria mystery,

NONNA MARIA

and the Case of the Stolen Necklace

COMING SOON FROM BANTAM BOOKS

1.

SHE WAS FOUND with her back against the side of a pine tree. Dust and scattered cones nestled along the backs of her folded legs, thick strands of dark hair partially covering her face. One of her arms was leaning against the base of the tree and the other was laid out flat, fingers resting on the edge of the curved road. She was motionless, her eyes closed, her lips slightly parted. A gentle wind ruffled her blue flowered dress, and one of her high-heeled shoes hung loose off her right foot.

It was seven in the morning on what would be another brutally hot summer day in Ischia, the sun rising above the calm waters of the port several miles below, its angled rays slowly beginning to wrap the woman in a blanket of warmth.

Two carabinieri officers parked their motorcycles at an angle to block off access to the road, patiently waiting for the medical examiner to arrive before allowing the body to be removed. A small group had gathered across the way—men and women who had been preparing to open their shops or head to work, stopped by the sight of the body of a woman none seemed to recognize.

The younger of the officers stared at the body, a concerned

look on his boyish face. "There's no blood anywhere," he said in a low voice. "It's almost as if she fell over and went to sleep."

"A sleep that lasts forever," the other officer said, stepping next to the young carabiniere. "Most likely a heart attack did her in. From the looks of it, she's been here a few hours. That puts the time of death in the middle of the night. Where would she be going? There's nothing around here at that hour but shuttered shops and a gas station. Closest house is at least a mile down the road."

A carabinieri car came up behind them, braking to a stop in front of the two motorcycles. The two officers turned from the woman's body and waited for their captain to approach them.

Captain Paolo Murino nodded at them and gave a quick glance at the group on the far side of the road. He stepped closer to the dead woman, his eyes taking in the curled body and the spot where she had come to rest. "Who called it in?" he asked, without turning his head.

"Local fruit peddler," the younger officer said. "Told me he was driving past on his way down from his farm, his truck packed with deliveries."

"Did he stop to check on her?" Captain Murino asked.

"No, sir," the officer said. "He gave her only a passing look, thought she might have had too much to drink and fallen asleep. He was running late."

"Did he leave you a name?"

The younger carabiniere pulled a notebook from his jacket pocket and flipped several pages. "Caldani," he said. "Bernardo Caldani."

"Check him out, make sure he is what he says he is," Murino said, staring at the younger of the two. "Your first week in Ischia, Franco, and you get to work a homicide. I'm certain that's not what you expected when you were transferred from Rome. Like anyone else who does a tour on the island, you were looking forward to days filled with quiet street patrols and flirting with tourists."

"What makes you so certain it was a homicide?" the second officer asked.

"Well, for one thing, her body would be at rest at that angle only if she had a number of broken bones," Captain Murino said. "I'm sure even you took note of that, Enrico."

"Yes, sir, I did," Enrico said. "But she could have fallen, tripped, and landed hard enough to break a bone or two."

"Perhaps," Captain Murino said, moving away from the two officers and standing in the center of the road. "But those two black skid marks tell me otherwise. If you compare them to the others on the road, you'll notice they are darker and deeper. That tells me they're fresh. Which might mean the woman's body was dumped or tossed from a car. She hit the ground hard, causing additional damage to her body."

"She is someone without a name," Franco said. "We didn't want to touch the body until the medical examiner signed off, but we looked for a bag or a purse and there wasn't any to be found."

"She has a name," Captain Murino said. "We just don't know it yet."

He turned to gaze out at the harbor below, where the first of the morning tourist boats were starting to head out for their trip around the island, and a packed hydrofoil was coming in to drop off another batch of guests. It was the second week of July and the tourists had been arriving in numbers far greater than in any previous year. Murino had been stationed in Ischia for six years now and was still surprised by the thousands who flocked to the island each season. Ischia, eighteen miles off the Naples coast, had been, since the late 1960s, a prime vacation destination for a devoted number of Italian, German, British, and American tourists who packed its many restaurants and beaches and enjoyed the supposedly healing powers of the thermal spas spread across the large island.

Captain Murino was in his mid-thirties, slim, with light brown razor-cut hair and, when the occasion called for it, a warm and engaging smile. He was set to marry a local girl in the fall, weeks after the last of the tourists had left the island, and he planned to make Ischia his permanent home, providing his superiors didn't have another transfer in mind. He was a Northern Italian who had grown to love the island and its many customs and traditions but was still regarded with suspicion by many of the locals. Over time, he was ever so slowly building up goodwill and trust among people who gave out such feelings with great reluctance.

"Canvass the area, talk to as many of the locals as you can," he said to the two officers. "Focus on the ones who live close by. Maybe one or two heard something or, with luck, saw something. Perhaps they might have a clue as to who this woman is or where she came from."

"Not exactly a pleasant way to begin a new day," Enrico

said, looking back at the crowd, grown larger since he had first come onto the scene.

Captain Murino looked at Enrico for a moment and then turned and stared at the body of the dead woman lying on the side of the quiet road. "Or to end one," he said in a low voice.

2.

NONNA MARIA STOOD in front of the glass butcher's counter in the open-air market of the port. It was early morning and the large space was already filled with shoppers, mostly locals buying what they needed for the afternoon meal and a handful of tourists who wandered through more out of curiosity than need. Behind the counter, a tall young man was running a thick slab of prosciutto through the slicing machine.

"I like it thin, Raphael," Nonna Maria said to the young man. "But not so thin that the slices stick to the paper. That happened to me last time I was here. Took more time to free the slices than it did to make the panini."

"It's not my fault, Nonna Maria," Raphael said with a smile. "This machine has a mind of its own. It cuts the way it wants to cut."

"Then you should put the machine aside and cut the slices with a knife," Nonna Maria said. "The way your father used to do. He had a surgeon's touch."

"It was easier for him to pay attention to his work," Raphael said, gazing around the crowded market. "There were fewer distractions back when he stood behind this counter."

"Your father didn't have time for distractions," Nonna Maria said. "He had a family to feed and a business to run. You'll understand one day. Once you're married and have children of your own."

"He was never happier than when he was behind this counter," Raphael said. "He didn't think of it as a job. It was more like he was spending his days in the company of his friends."

"We felt the same way about him," Nonna Maria said. "It was a different island in those years. It's a much richer place now, our summers filled with tourists eager to spend money. And that makes it easier for our young men and women to earn a good living. But I miss those quiet days more and more. I suppose it is all part of getting old. But it's nice to keep memories of friends alive. Friends like your father."

"He said you were the one who talked him out of opening a restaurant and into setting up a butcher shop instead," Raphael said.

"It was more my husband, Gabriel, than me," Nonna Maria said. "But I agreed. Fabrizio hated crowds, and if a restaurant isn't crowded it goes out of business. But he loved talking to people and was a great salesman. And he made a success out of being a butcher. He worked hard and I never once saw him without a smile on his face."

Raphael wrapped the prosciutto in brown paper and taped the packet down on both ends. "I know you asked for a kilo," he said to Nonna Maria. "But I gave you a kilo and a half."

"Only if you let me pay for it," Nonna Maria said.

Raphael stepped out from behind the counter and rested a

hand on Nonna Maria's shoulder. "Think of it as a gift," he said. "Not from me. From my father."

Nonna Maria smiled and nodded. "In that case, I thank you both," she said. "You for the kind gesture and your father for the delicious gift."

3.

ARIANNA CONTE RAN out of room 226 of the Grand Hotel Excelsior and bounded down two flights of stairs, bumping her hip against the curled iron railing just before reaching the entryway. She made a sharp left turn and came to a full stop at the front desk and slammed both her hands on the counter. She was short of breath, and a sheen of sweat coated her face and arms.

"I need to speak to the manager," she said, her voice echoing throughout the lobby. "And I need to speak to him now!"

"He's on a long-distance call at the moment," the young woman behind the counter said, speaking in a mellow voice, looking to calm an agitated guest. "Is there anything I can do to help?"

"You can go inside and tell him to hang up on that call and get out here," Arianna Conte said, in an even louder tone of voice. "And then you can put in a call to the police and have them here as soon as possible."

"The police?" the young woman said. "Why do you want me to call the police?"

"Why?" Arianna shouted. "I'll tell you why! My necklace was stolen from out of my room! A very valuable necklace, one that has been in my family for generations, handed down to me by my own mother."

"Are you sure you didn't misplace it?" the young woman behind the counter asked.

Arianna stared at the girl for a moment, her anger rising. She read the name on the tag pinned to the young woman's white blouse. "I do not misplace anything, Branka," she said. "Especially something as valuable as that necklace. Now, do as I asked you to do. Get the manager and call the police. That woman needs to be arrested before she has a chance to leave the hotel."

"What woman?"

"What do you mean, what woman?" Arianna said, slamming a fist on the counter. "The one who stole my necklace! A member of your cleaning crew. She's been sniffing after that necklace since I checked in earlier this week. I had my suspicions about her, but I kept them to myself. If I had only acted sooner, none of this would have occurred."

"Did you see her take it?" Branka asked.

"I didn't have to witness it to know she's the one who stole it," Arianna said. "She's in my room morning, afternoon, and night. Waits until I leave for a meal or head to the beach. Always watching. And when I return, my things have always been moved, never where I left them. Including my necklace, there, in plain sight, for her to see and to take."

"Why did you not make use of the safe in your room?" Branka asked.

"A child could break open that safe," Arianna said. "I've been in many five-star hotels in my travels and have never kept

anything in any safe. That's the first place a thief looks when he—or, in this case, she—is looking to steal."

The hotel manager opened the door behind Branka and quietly stepped up to the counter. He was thin, of average height, with salt-and-pepper hair cropped short. He was wearing a crisp white shirt, open at the collar, and he stood directly across from Arianna. "I couldn't help but overhear," he said in a soothing voice. "The door to the office is not thick, as you can see."

"Then you are well aware that my precious necklace was stolen," Arianna said.

"I am well aware that you claim your necklace is missing," the hotel manager said. "And I assure you, we will not rest until it is found."

"She says someone on the cleaning staff has taken it," Branka said.

"So I understand," the hotel manager said. "Do you know the name of the alleged thief? You've said you've seen her multiple times, so I would imagine you got a look at her name tag, just as you are now looking at mine."

"Yes, Antonio," Arianna said. "I can describe her *and* name her. For you and for the police. Her name is Loretta, a petite young woman, always with an annoying smile on her face."

Antonio stood quietly for a few moments, looking at Arianna, her multicolored robe no doubt costing more than he earned in a month, thick curls of blond hair hanging down the sides of her face. She was in her mid-sixties, he guessed, and looked it, despite the daily herbal treatments meant to give her

a more youthful appearance. This was her first stay at his hotel, unlike many of the other guests who returned season after season, making the Excelsior their yearly retreat.

"And you have no doubt it was Loretta who stole your necklace?" Antonio asked.

"None whatsoever," Arianna said.

"I heard you tell Branka that the necklace has been in your family for generations," Antonio said. "I assume, then, that it's not an inexpensive piece of jewelry."

Arianna leaned over the counter, inches from Antonio, and spoke in a lower voice, tinged with rage. "It is worth more than the meager amount you and your staff could earn in a lifetime," she said.

Antonio nodded and turned to Branka. "Please put in a call to the carabinieri," he said to her. "Tell them we have a guest who wishes to report a theft. And then send one of the bellboys to go find Nonna Maria and ask her to come here as soon as she can."

"Why Nonna Maria?" Branka asked.

Antonio turned to Arianna and smiled. "For many reasons," he said to Branka. "Prime among them is that Loretta is Nonna Maria's goddaughter. Which means this incident will be of great interest to her."

"Who is this Nonna Maria?" Arianna asked, not bothering to hide her frustration.

"If there has indeed been a theft," Antonio said, "she will be a great help to the police in finding the thief and returning the necklace to you."

"Is she a police officer?" Arianna asked.

Antonio shook his head. "No, Nonna Maria is not a member of the carabinieri," he said.

"What is she, then?"

"Nonna Maria is simply a friend," Antonio said. "A very good friend."

PHOTO: © KATE CARCATERRA

LORENZO CARCATERRA is the #1 *New York Times* bestselling author of *A Safe Place, Sleepers, Apaches, Gangster, Street Boys, Paradise City, Chasers, Midnight Angels, The Wolf, Tin Badges, Payback,* and *Three Dreamers*. He is a former writer/producer for *Law & Order* and has written for *National Geographic Traveler* and *The New York Times Magazine*. He lives in New York City.

lorenzocarcaterra.com